CHANGES

SUN VALLEY SERIES BOOK 3

KELLIE COATES GILBERT

Dedicated to my friend, Denise Page,
a woman who faced far too many changes in her life, yet held onto her
faith.

PRAISE FOR KELLIE COATES GILBERT

"If you're looking for a new author to read, you can't go wrong with Kellie Coates Gilbert."

— LISA WINGATE, NY TIMES BESTSELLING AUTHOR OF
WHEN WE WERE YOURS

"Gilbert's heartfelt fiction is always a pleasure to read."

— BUZZING FOR BOOKS

"Well-drawn, sympathetic characters and graceful language."

— LIBRARY JOURNAL

ALSO BY KELLIE COATES GILBERT

CHANGES

SUN VALLEY SERIES – BOOK 3

Kellie Coates Gilbert

1

Long before dawn crested over the mountains surrounding the resort town of Sun Valley, Idaho, Leigh Ann Blackburn pulled herself from rumpled sheets after yet another sleepless night.

With determination, she grabbed her Buscemi Ventura sneakers from the shelf in her closet, the lavender ones that perfectly matched the cute hoodie she'd snagged last fall.

There was a time when she'd never given a second thought to shelling out over six hundred dollars for a pair of sneakers. She could buy multiple pairs, if she'd wanted. That was no longer the case. Not after Mark's business snafu.

When the Prescott USA deal went south, they'd had to tighten their financial belts. Thank goodness for the dab of savings she'd been smart enough to put away. Still, their cash reserves would not hold out for long. Mark was going to have to scramble and find a way to generate income again—and soon.

She sat on her tufted closet chair and pulled the sneakers onto her feet and tied the shoestrings, recounting in her mind all the changes she'd seen in the past months, and the reasons she had to fret.

Joie, her youngest sister, had ended an affair with a man who had turned out to be a liar and an all-around jerk, only to find herself pregnant and now a mommy.

Karyn, her other sister, had hit a major wall in her relationship with Grayson when he'd learned he had a young son and had returned to Alaska to be a full-time father. Whether he would re-marry his ex-wife was a bit unclear. Even so, their relationship was over and Karyn was forced to move on.

Her middle sister rarely dwelt on hard things—she was a cup-half-full kind of girl. Still, this breakup had thrown her for a loop. She couldn't say she blamed Karyn for being angry. It had been hard for her to step into a new relationship after Dean died. Now, she'd suffered another loss and was alone again.

If all this wasn't enough to worry about, the day she'd been most dreading had arrived—the day her son, Colby, would have to report for duty. She'd been accused of being a helicopter mom, of hovering over her son far too much. The irony didn't escape her. Soon, he'd be climbing into one several continents away, potentially flying into harm's way.

She still could still not wrap her head around the fact her son had gone off and enlisted in the army—or that he'd shown up on their doorstep with a wife—a granola girl. An avowed vegetarian, her new daughter-in-law regularly shunned Leigh Ann's expensive shampoo, claiming baking soda a more natural way to wash her hair. She refused to take aspirin for her headaches, electing instead to rub peppermint oil on her temples. She didn't even shave her underarms and legs!

Leigh Ann could spend the next year trying to sort out why Colby had diverted from everything she'd hoped and dreamed of for him—but it wouldn't do her any good. What was done was done. The more important thing now was for him to get through these next months and see him come home safe and in one piece.

With that thought in mind, Leigh Ann finished dressing, then made her way out to the garage where she slipped into her waiting SUV. As soon as she turned the engine, the radio blared.

And we expect another warm summer day here in Sun Valley as residents in this popular resort area prepare to welcome dozens of the world's most influential people arriving in the coming weeks to attend Vanguard, an annual event where media stars and business moguls forge relationships and make deals in comfort and secrecy.

She turned the radio off, not needing a reminder of how demanding the weeks ahead would be. Which is why she was heading up Baldy for an early morning hike, to clear her head of the chaos.

She'd invited Karyn along, but as expected, her sister had declined the offer. She'd never been up on the mountain since—well, since her husband's fatal accident.

The parking lot at the River Run Day Lodge was nearly vacant except for two vehicles with empty bike racks on top. Leigh Ann parked in the spot closest to the foot bridge that spanned the Wood River.

Sun Valley was a world-class ski resort known best as a winter destination, yet summer remained Leigh Ann's favorite season. She loved the warm days and cool nights, burbling clear-water brooks and wildflowers sprinkled across the mountain side, the concerts and farmer's markets in outdoor venues—she adored it all.

While the season had lived up to her expectations, the events in her life and in those she loved had fallen far short.

A walk would no doubt do her good, help her put all the bad things out of her mind, at least for a little while.

After checking her fit-bit, Leigh Ann marched past the shops leading to the chair lift and headed up the packed dirt trail that briefly paralleled the Wood River before switching back up the sides of a heavily wooded shady valley. She tightened the lid on her stainless-steel water bottle, the views becoming increasingly more expansive the higher she climbed.

Despite her vow not to dwell on the fact Colby was leaving, her mind betrayed her. She could think of little else.

It was only yesterday, it seemed, that she was a young mother in bed, so tired she couldn't wake, couldn't move. Colby had the croup and she'd spent the better part of the night holding him while sitting on the toilet in a steamy bathroom.

She was exhausted and in a deep sleep—and then, the bed moved, ever so slightly. She tried to ignore the motion, but within seconds the bed jostled even more. She'd pried one eye open, praying it was nothing and hoping to catch more much-needed sleep, even if only ten minutes.

Her luck ran out.

The bed moved again. Soon, a tiny head popped into view. Colby's hair was sticking up all over, at least the parts that weren't glued to his head from sweating.

"Wade up, Mommy. Wade up," he said. *"I hundry."*

Children cry, all the time, nonstop. They never sleep. They're terrible conversationalists. And, they take everything you've got. All your time. All your patience. All your focus. All your sleep— everything, until you've got nothing left.

But when little Colby put his nose up against her own that morning, his cold little nose, and he said, *"I wub you, Mommy"*— oh, the love she'd felt, an irrational, unbridled deep affection for her son.

And now her beloved boy was all grown up and had enlisted. She should be proud he was serving his country, and she was. She was also filled with dread and terror unlike anything she'd ever known.

The sun was up now, warming the air. Leigh Ann removed her hoodie and tied it around her waist before climbing higher, past groves of aspens alternating with deep pine-scented ever-greens. A man on a bicycle pedaled past, waved. She nodded back.

It wasn't long before she hit the junction and headed up the foot-traffic-only Roundhouse Connector trail, past the Louis Stur memorial and water fountain. She stopped and filled her water bottle before making the trek to the crest where she'd climb onto the ski lift and ride back down the mountain.

At the top, Leigh Ann sank to the ground ready to enjoy her reward—a three-hundred-sixty-degree magnificent view in all directions.

All her problems, including Colby's leaving, seemed to shrink against the vast vistas before her—the jagged Pioneer and Sawtooth mountain ranges, the sprawling valley below with everything in miniature. She could barely make out the Sun Valley Lodge, the stables and golf course, or even her own house.

Leigh Ann sat cross-legged, taking it all in for nearly an hour before the dials on her watch commanded her to stand and make her way to the chair lift. She'd remain longer if she could. Unfortunately, she couldn't escape returning to the valley below—and to all the changes that awaited.

2

The baby was crying.

Joie woke with a start and bolted upright in bed.

The baby was crying!

Without bothering to push away the sweaty hair glued to her face, she shoved the tangle of sheets from her legs and bolted for the cradle. On the way, she stubbed her toe on the dirty spaghetti bowl she'd left on the floor from the night before, spilling the remaining food onto the carpet.

She let out an expletive, immediately wishing she could gobble the words back. It didn't matter that little Hudson was only a few weeks old. All the books said that infants absorb their surroundings, even at this age.

As if on auto pilot, her arms scooped her baby son from his bed and she brought him to her shoulder and patted his backside, trying to calm him. Until days ago, she'd have refuted the notion any woman could sleep while standing. Unfortunately, she'd learned new mothers often pulled off stunts unknown to mankind.

"Shhh, shhhh—you can't be hungry already, Little Man." She

pried an eye open and glanced at the wall clock. "It hasn't even been two hours."

At that moment, she remembered her plan to return to work this morning. Proud of the fact she only required three weeks of maternity leave, she'd hushed her critics—especially her oldest sister, Leigh Ann.

"There's no reason I can't go back to work already. Maddy and I made arrangements. I'll be taking little Hudson to the office with me. We both know babies sleep most of the time at this age. There's no reason he can't do that in a crib just feet from my desk while I work," she'd argued, choosing to cut her sister off when she tried to warn her about erratic sleep schedules and the exhaustion that might bring.

"No one ever choked to death by swallowing her pride and listening to good advice," Leigh Ann told her. For that reason alone, Joie would rather change a thousand dirty diapers than admit her sister was right—which is why she groaned when her phone rang and Leigh Ann's face appeared on the caller display.

Joie sank into the rocking chair and reached for the phone. Bringing it to her ear without waking Hudson proved a challenge, but if she let the call go to voicemail Leigh Ann would likely show up on her doorstep within ten minutes to see what was wrong.

"Hello," she answered, her tired voice camouflaged with as much brightness as she could muster.

"Hey." Surprisingly, Leigh Ann's voice encompassed its own hint of weariness. "I know you have a lot going on these days, but I wanted to remind you about Colby's farewell party."

"Oh no, is that tonight?"

"Yes, at seven. You don't have to bring a thing—just yourself and my little nephew. Oh, and make sure Clint knows he's welcome."

"We're not a couple, Leigh Ann," she pointed out, again. Her sister was like a dog with a bone—a strong-willed German shepherd who had decided her former boss, a cowboy who ran the

Sun Valley Stables, was the perfect husband candidate for her wayward baby sister.

Despite their rocky start, Clint Ladner had proven he could be a good friend. He never judged her, or her impulsive choices. Instead, he was quietly there, offering support and friendship.

He definitely had a lot to offer in that "manly" department too. She had to admit when she'd first met him in Crusty's over a game of pool, she'd admired the way he wore that tight pair of jeans, the way he rolled up his shirt sleeves to reveal a bear tattoo on his forearm. At the same time, he'd had a disconcerting way of looking at her. She felt naked under the weight of his stare, exposed.

Over time, his scrutiny became less bothersome. She was exposed—yes—but it was an amazing thing when someone really sees you.

Clint Ladner wasn't like a lot of the guys she'd hooked up with. He had a surprising soft side. Besides her sisters, he was the one person she learned she could count on. He was her friend. A stranger she'd known all her life.

Why risk that kind of companionship by jumping into bed together—turn what they had into a relationship that would, in all likelihood, torpedo in the end, leaving their friendship decimated?

What would she be left with then?

Leigh Ann pushed. "Don't be stubborn. Invite him. I'm sure Clint would love to join us."

Joie rolled her eyes. She was simply too tired to argue. "I'll see," she promised, in that way you do when you have no intention of following through.

"Never mind. I'll call him," Leigh Ann told her.

Joie was forming an argument when she heard a light rap at the door. Puzzled, and a little alarmed, she wondered who could be stopping by at this early hour. "Look, I've got to go. There's someone at my door."

"Who shows up at your house this early?"

Joie sighed. "I don't know, Leigh Ann. Let me off the phone and I'll go see and report back to you." She paused, aware she'd been overly snarky. Lack of sleep had intensified her inability to cope with her sister's intrusions. "Look, I'll see you tonight, okay? And I'll call Clint. I promise."

She hurried to end the call and moved for the entryway, peeked out the peephole on the door. She perked up slightly when she saw Clint standing there.

Juggling Hudson on one shoulder, Joie reached and opened the door, dismissing the momentary concern she had over the way she looked. She was pretty sure she'd worn this same pair of yoga pants for three days straight. "Hey, this is a surprise."

He smiled and held up a cardboard carrier loaded with Styrofoam cups of coffee and a bag. "I knew you were starting back at the office today and brought you breakfast. Figured you might not have your morning routine quite down yet—and from the looks of your hair and the time on that wall clock, I was right."

She glanced at the time. "Oh no! I'm late. Can you take him?" She shoved the baby into his arms. "I have to jump in the shower, now!"

He grinned and maneuvered little Hudson into a secure place in the crook of his arm and slid the goodies he'd brought onto the kitchen counter. He lifted a cup toward her. "At least drink your coffee."

She grabbed the cup and ran for the bathroom, looked back over her shoulder, "By the way, I didn't get a chance to get over to the ATM. Can you lend me some cash?"

He gave her an amused smile, reached in his pocket and pulled out a small roll of bills, peeled off a fifty.

"Thanks, just toss it in my purse." she hollered as she rounded the corner into her bedroom.

See? That's what she was talking about. Clint Ladner was the kind of friend you could bank on.

3

Karyn strode toward the entry to the Sun Valley Lodge wishing she could have stayed home in bed. Not even the swans gracefully gliding across the pond out front could lift her mood this morning.

It'd been three weeks, four days, six hours, ten calorie-filled milkshakes (five chocolate and five vanilla) over two dozen candy bars and two large bags of red twizzler licorice since Grayson had left and returned to Alaska with his wife—well, ex-wife—and their adorable little brown-haired son, a boy who looked so like Grayson it made her heart ache.

Heartbreak was a real thing. She could raise her right hand and testify to that fact. She'd experienced a fractured heart twice.

First, she'd lost Dean. She'd barely survived the aftermath of his accidental death. Then she'd met someone new—a back country pilot with a smile that made her melt. Just when she had a reason for climbing out of bed each morning, when she'd finally removed her wedding ring believing she could fall in love and start over, Grayson had single-handedly imploded her world yet again.

Why hadn't she fought to keep him? Worked harder to

convince him to parent long distance? He had a plane, for goodness sakes. He could have used it regularly and flown back and forth. Like a milquetoast who was afraid to stand up for herself, she'd failed to put up any strong argument. Instead, she'd simply acquiesced to a woman who showed up to steal him away from her—a woman with a history of grinding his heart with her stiletto heels.

What was wrong with her that she was willing to let that happen?

Karyn marched to the front door, wishing she could turn the clock back, do it all differently.

"Good morning, Karyn." The white-gloved doorman opened the heavy door and waved her inside. "See you at the Huddle."

The Huddle was the official name given to the early morning employee meeting held down in the newly renovated bowling alley in the basement level of the lodge. When she'd come on board as the Director of Hospitality, the employees often teased her by renaming it the Cuddle, based on her inclusive and upbeat style.

This morning, Karyn wasn't entirely sure the label fit. Her attitude was anything but warm and fuzzy.

At her desk, she gathered the reservation sheets and agendas for the upcoming Vanguard conference. Soon, the lodge would be bustling with activity—and VIPs. Security would be tight. And it would be her job to make sure everything ran smoothly and with no hitches.

The Sun Valley Lodge had a storied history. As the centerpiece of America's original ski resort, the lodge first opened in 1936. Wood pillars and floors graced the lobby, along with thick plush rugs. Local art and massive windows overlooked an ice skating rink where Olympians often practiced. *"Roughing it in Luxury"* the travel brochures claimed.

She'd been thrilled to land this job. In many ways, the confidence Jon Sebring had shown in her abilities had saved her as she tried to climb out of the darkness following Dean's death.

She certainly couldn't let Jon down now. She'd simply have to focus—no matter how much her heart ached.

Armed with this determined attitude and a stack of files, she lifted her chin and headed into battle—or in this case, a meeting of hungry employees who would no doubt be sad to learn she'd neglected to stop and pick up the donuts.

Their staff meetings were held in the newly renovated basement of the Lodge that sported a six-lane bowling alley and game room area with bright orange banquettes and stools. Despite the distant noise coming from the kitchen, the atmosphere was upbeat and lent to the mood she liked to maintain.

"Hey everyone, thanks for coming," she said, opening the meeting. "We've got a lot to do today, so let's make this brief." She handed out the packets she'd put together. "As you know, we have the Vanguard conference starting very soon."

Jess Barnett, their new sous chef, slid into one of the brightly-colored plastic seats. "Yeah, I already spotted a Learjet at the airport this morning."

His new wife, Lindsay, who now ran the gift shop, added, "Let's hope one of those rich jet owners will make their way into the gift shop and buy one of my jewelry pieces."

The young couple exchanged smiles.

"I'm sure I don't have to remind you that Vanguard maintains a cloak of secrecy. Take a look at page five in your packet. This outlines the security measures that we are putting in place. The lodge will be closed to the general public during the conference. At no time will photographs or recordings be allowed. As an employee of the resort, you are not to disclose the identities of any of our guests, or discuss anything related to the attendees outside these walls."

Melissa Jacquard, their very pregnant desk clerk, raised her hand. "Will there be a list of approved vendors? Last year we had a guy show up in a plumber's jumpsuit telling me he was here to unplug a toilet."

"Let me guess—" said one of the maids. "His plunger was really a hidden camera and he intended to sneak out more than a wad of nasty hair pulled from the drain?"

Karyn held up her open hands. "Yes, there will be a lot of interest in this conference. People will use any means possible to gain access to the attendees. Let's keep our eyes open." She turned to Melissa. "And to answer your question, no vendor will be allowed inside without my personal approval." She looked at the doormen. "Period."

There were other questions, mainly relating to how they would divide up duties relating to the increased workload. The kitchen staff seemed to have the expanded menus under control. Likewise, housekeeping was staffed to handle a full house.

When the meeting finally concluded in the bowling alley, she gathered her files and headed back to her office. She hadn't made it past the door when Melissa stopped her.

"Hey, a few of us are going to dinner at the Sawtooth Club tomorrow night. We'd love for you and Grayson to join us."

The invite might as well have been one of those heavy balls, bowling Karyn over and sending her emotions into the gutter lane. "I—I can't." She fought to inhale, surprised news hadn't gotten out. "Uh, Grayson is—I mean—we broke up."

She didn't make it a practice to discuss personal issues with her employees, but this warranted a bit of clarification. It was better to just clear everything up right now. "He moved back to Alaska."

Her co-worker's face filled with empathy. "Oh, Karyn—I'm so sorry. I didn't know." Melissa placed her hand on her forearm. "But, you can still come if you want."

Karyn shook her head. "I'm sorry. I already have another commitment." Never mind the commitment was to slip into bed and pull the covers over her head. "Another time?"

"Yeah, sure."

Karyn hurried out. At the first opportunity, she ducked into the stairwell, took the stairs two at a time until she reached the landing leading to the main level. Pulling the heavy metal door open, she stepped into the empty hallway, glanced both ways before slipping into the electrical closet, pulling the heavy door closed behind her.

In the darkness, she let the tears flow. Tears of sadness—of anger.

She slumped against the cold wall and puddled onto the concrete floor, next to a mop and bucket, the aroma dank and smelling mildly of antiseptic soap.

Her hands dug into her pocket for her phone.

She should call him—give him a piece of her mind. Did he even know what he'd done by leaving her alone to deal with this loss?

Her thumb scrolled through her contacts until his name appeared. Before dialing, she took a deep breath, paused. What would she say exactly?

Worse, his little son's face formed in her mind.

Her lip quivered as she slowly pressed the off button, leaving the face of her phone to go dark.

She drew a deep breath. She would not call him—not now, and likely not ever. He'd made his decision and she was left with accepting that he'd chosen Robin and that little boy over her—perhaps rightfully so.

She just wished someone would remind her heart that Grayson had noble intentions that extended beyond hurting her.

Karyn closed her eyes, leaned her head against the hard wall. With little effort, she could remember the way he smelled when she nested her face against his neck—a clean scent mixed with spicy aftershave that, frankly, used to make her knees quiver.

She recalled the way his beard stubble felt against her fingers, how he looked in a collared shirt and jeans—the smile he wore that first time he took her to dinner at the Ram. They were both so nervous. As the evening progressed, it easily became apparent they were a fit. They were good together, really good—like Nutella spread thick over a slice of bread fresh from the oven good.

Tears bloomed fresh in her eyes.

She tired of this heartache—of having the men she loved snatched away, leaving her in wounded pieces. All she wanted right now was to feel—well, to feel nothing. For just a little while.

Her hands dug inside her purse. She suffered an occasional migraine, and kept a couple of prescription tablets tucked inside to alleviate any sudden onset of pain over-the-counter medications rarely eliminated.

A small voice inside her head warned against the unthinkable, still her fingers searched for the bottle. The way she figured, even an emotional void was better than this kind of pain.

She pulled the tiny container from her bag and emptied the contents into the palm of her hand, wishing she had some water to wash them down. Two might be too many, so she decided to take just one of the pills.

Without another thought, Karyn tossed the tablet inside her mouth and swallowed. She closed her eyes and waited.

Her conscience should kick in and feel something—guilt, perhaps? Strangely, no remorse appeared. Instead, for the first time in weeks, she felt powerful. She alone controlled her emotions. No man—no situation.

Within a few short minutes, the hole inside her filled—this time with barren resignation.

4

A fter finishing her hike, Leigh Ann trekked across the parking lot and climbed back in her SUV, feeling a little more ready to face the day ahead. Despite the emotional toll the day would demand, she'd do what she always did—she'd simply move forward and accomplish what had to be done.

The first thing on her long list was to stop at Konditori and pick up the food for tonight. When Mark worried about the expense, she'd taken a couple of her favorite rings and sold them incognito on eBay. There'd be time for tightening their budget later, but not tonight. This party had to be the perfect sendoff for her boy, and she wouldn't scrimp.

Her sisters had chastised her for the extravagance. "Did you have to invite the whole town?" Joie asked. "I mean, sure— include family and our closest friends. But, don't you think a guest list that rivals an Oscar after-party might be a little much?" Her sister Karyn had agreed. "I'm not sure Colby wants to spend his last night with all these people."

Leigh Ann brushed off their concerns. "My boy is leaving to

serve his country—these people. I want them to all know about his sacrifice, and honor it."

Okay, yes—that was partially the truth. Deep down, she also wanted them to see the sacrifice she and Mark were making. Perhaps that fact might reverse some of the damage Mark had done with the Prescott USA deal.

No doubt, there were a lot of people still smarting over nearly losing their livelihoods. Rumor had it, the cost to the employees had been substantial. When faced with Mark and Andrea's takeover plan, they'd engaged in a tactic known as the poison pill, which required immense funding. They'd collectively liquidated large blocks of their 401Ks in order to save their company—and their jobs.

She needed to do something to weasel back into their good graces—even if it meant flaunting the fact her son was leaving to serve in a dangerous place in order to keep their hineys safe.

She wondered, not for the first time, what Colby would be eating while over there. And, where he'd sleep. In one of those horribly uncomfortable cots, like the ones she'd seen in the movies? Would he have some foul-mouthed superior screaming at him for not squaring the corners sufficiently when making up his bed? Would he even get enough sleep?

Would he be shot at?

She squirmed a little, tried to push the terrifying thought from her mind. If she continued to dwell on all the possibilities, she'd never make it through the next hours—or the months ahead.

Leigh Ann started the car and wove her way out of the parking lot, thinking instead about her perfectly planned menu. After careful consideration, she'd elected to go with finger foods passed by servers. This would help people mingle. She hated it when people congregated at a crowded food table.

She'd gone with Asian-themed selections since Colby was going to Korea. There'd be coconut shrimp drizzled with a delicious sauce made of pineapple with a touch of jalapenos for some kick, Thai green curry hot wings, delicate tender-steamed snow peas with sesame seeds, roasted chicken skewers with peanut sauce, and pork and kimchi dumplings.

Just the thought of all that delicious food made Leigh Ann's stomach growl as she waited for the traffic to clear before turning right onto Main Street.

She'd also be serving a distinct cocktail known as the Lotus Blossom made with pear-flavored vodka and Japanese sake in pretty martini glasses rimmed with ground lychee nuts, sugar and lime.

She hadn't meant to go overboard, but this was a special occasion that deserved the very best.

Minutes later, she eased into a parking space directly behind the area known as the mall—a group of shops in the center of Sun Valley and only walking distance from the lodge.

The Konditori was already packed with tourists who had no doubt heard this was the best place for breakfast. A little girl in a pretty red bow sat at a table across from her family, scooping whipped cream with her finger from a swan shaped crème puff dusted with powdered sugar.

Leigh Ann made her way to the counter and waved at the owner.

From inside the kitchen, he wiped his hands on a big white towel tucked inside the band of his apron and headed her way. "Leigh Ann, glad you stopped by. I'm afraid we have a bit of an issue that has developed."

Her eyebrows shot up. "An issue?"

He placed his hand on her arm and guided her to a back room that contained large plastic food containers on metal shelving. "I'm afraid your credit card was denied."

A sick feeling filled her gut. Her hands went clammy, her ears rang a little. "Denied?"

The owner looked horribly uncomfortable. He nodded. "I'm afraid so."

Leigh Ann felt almost feverish with worry. "But, I have a party and—"

"Yes, I know. And I don't want you to worry. We've got you covered. You've a long history with us, been one of our best customers. I know you're good for the money."

Relief flooded her addled mind. "Oh—" She let out a long breath. "I—I don't know what to say. Except, thank you. I mean it, and I will make sure you are paid in full right away."

"Yeah, I know. We're good."

She nodded. "Yes, good."

Back in the car, Leigh Ann planted her face against the steering wheel. Never had she been so humiliated! She'd sold her rings, put the money into their household account. There should have been plenty of funds to cover her purchases.

Angry, she pulled her phone from her bag, dialed Mark and told him what had happened. She could almost hear him deflate over the phone. "I'm sorry, honey. I knew this might come. Evidently, all our accounts have been frozen, pending the outcome of the litigation against us. From now on, we'll have to use cash."

"But what do I do now? How do I pay for this bill?" She knew her raised voice wasn't going to help solve the situation, but he'd made this mess. He needed to provide a solution—and fast.

Her husband must've noted the panic in her voice. "Don't worry," he told her. "I'll see to it the bill is paid somehow."

Reluctantly, she thanked him and hung up, then grabbed her key fob and pressed the ignition button. This situation with the bill was all she'd needed this morning. Now she was running late, and she still had to stop by and pick up the baskets of lilies from Hamilton's Nursery. Thank goodness she'd already paid Dee Dee's invoice.

After checking the rearview mirror, she placed the car in

reverse and proceeded to back out. Immediately, she heard a horrible noise—a thumping sound.

She groaned. Oh no—not a flat!

Leigh Ann jumped from the car and glanced at the front tire. Flat. Likewise the back tire on the driver's side. Flat.

She scurried around to the other side to find all the tires deflated. Every one of them—flat as a pancake.

That's when she knew—this was no accident.

5

F rom the dining alcove off her kitchen, Leigh Ann watched the party preparations taking place. Mark stood at the entertainment system and adjusted the volume on the music. The bartenders iced down beer and opened bottles of wine. The caterers loaded up trays with hors d'oeuvres while the wait staff stood by ready to begin their duties.

Everything was ready, provided anyone actually showed up.

RSVPs had been slow to roll in. Andrea and Dee Dee Hamiliton were the first to reply, saying they were looking forward to the evening and the chance to give Colby their best. Nash Billingsley and Marley from down at the butcher shop in Atkinson's Market both assured her they'd be attending. Of course, the Dilworth sisters assured her they would never miss it.

There were others, but there was also a long list of people she hadn't heard from. She'd passed the issue off as bad manners, or lack of time or just plain forgetting to respond. After today's tire incident, she now wondered if it might be something more.

"Don't worry," Joie told her, cradling little Hudson in the crook of her arm. "Besides, if nobody shows, who cares? More for us to eat and drink."

Her father was quick to join in. "She's right, sweetheart. Besides, this whole thing will blow over soon. People rarely stay mad for long. Another thing will come along and pull their attention and they'll forget all about this Preston, USA deal."

Leigh Ann wasn't so sure he was right. By her calculations, there had been a lot of instances where a kind of mob mentality blossomed and took over. Rumors spread, many of them complete untruths. Just as often, people hardened their hearts and forgiveness was rarely contemplated.

True, it was only a matter of time before she knew whether the storm Mark had created would turn into a social tornado and devastate her standing in this community. By the looks of the empty seating in her living room, she was about to experience at least a category four hit.

KARYN SAT in her car with the radio softly playing a Fleetwood Mac tune. The band had been around long before she'd hit her teens, but the band was still a favorite.

> *Well, I've been afraid of changin'*
> *'Cause I've built my life around you*

THOSE LYRICS CERTAINLY RANG TRUE—MORE so today than ever. She'd built her life around needing companionship. She hated sleeping alone in a big empty bed, placing a single plate on the table at dinnertime, not having anyone sitting on the sofa next to her watching Saturday Night Live reruns on television. Rosanne Rosannadanna wasn't quite as funny when you had no one to laugh with.

She looked at the cars lined up and down the street. Not as

many as she'd expected, but each vehicle represented another potential encounter where she'd have to face sympathetic stares and whispered worries over whether or not she'd make it past another loss. Why must she always be the victim—the sad one? More, when would the emptiness inside finally be filled?

The radio station changed and another song came on, some sappy tune about falling in love. She reached and turned it off, sighed and reached for her purse.

She couldn't face listening to lyrics extolling the magic of falling in love, and she couldn't face that party. Not feeling this raw.

Karyn dug inside her bag and found the pill bottle, opened it and popped a single tablet into her mouth. Tomorrow, she'd cope. But, not tonight.

Tonight, with the help from that tiny pill, she'd paste on the happy smile everyone expected. She'd be charming and chatty and happy. She'd laugh at people's jokes, tell the women they looked lovely and give her sisters big hugs—especially Leigh Ann, who would no doubt fall apart the minute the spotlight turned to Colby and his leaving.

She'd be there for her, just like the many times her oldest sister had supported her.

Armed with this resolve, Karyn climbed from her car and made her way to the front door. Family didn't need to ring the doorbell, so she simply walked in.

Miss Trudy spotted her. "Well, there you are!" The owner of the local art studio elbowed her way through the crowd. "Oh, baby. How are you?"

"I'm fine," Karyn lied. Taking a step back, she pointed at Miss Trudy's feet, changed the subject. "Where did you get those gorgeous shoes? I love leopard print," she said, lying again. She hated leopard print, thought it was cheap looking and too busy. Somehow, though, Miss Trudy pulled off the look.

Miss Trudy brought her hand to her chest, sending her

bangle bracelets clattering. "Oh, these? I found them at Panache. A little spendy, but I traded for a hammered silver wrist cuff I made." Her face went all soft. "But enough about my shoes, dear. How *are* you?" She reached and pulled Karyn into her ample bosom, nearly suffocating her in a cloud of rich, musky perfume. "Grayson leaving you is just awful—just plain awful."

She tried to pull back, had a hard time untangling her hair from Miss Trudy's dangling earrings. "Like I said. I'm fine. Really."

Karyn spotted Joie and waved. "Oh, you'll have to excuse me. I have a little nephew I'm dying to hold."

She moved quickly in that direction, and almost made it. Unfortunately, she was intercepted by Tessa McCreary, the realtor who sold Grayson his house up Warm Springs. "Oh, Karyn—I was so stunned to hear Grayson's voicemail telling me he was moving back to Alaska."

"Voicemail?"

"Yes," she said. "He wanted me to list his house. I think he's going to make a tidy profit, even in the short time he owned that property."

Karyn's heart thudded against her chest. So, he really was cutting all ties to the area. She'd known that, but somewhere deep inside she'd hoped there might be a chance he'd wake up and change his mind.

"I remember when I showed him that house," Tess said. "He was so reluctant to consider anything in that price range, that is until you pointed out the special amenities."

She remembered. The home consisted of two levels, the bottom floor a large open area with vaulted ceilings and massive windows overlooking a stand of quaking aspens in full splendor lining a brook.

Overhead was a loft. The railing of rough-hewn posts called to mind the early frontier days of this part of Idaho, when the Sun Valley area was a thriving silver mining town. Besides timber, glass, and stone, portions of the interior had the traditional look of square-cut logs and chinking—sturdy and dependable, like the house could protect the inhabitants from even the harshest winter.

She stared off into the kitchen where her sister was busy loading a platter with hor d'oeuvres. "Yes, the house was lovely."

A waiter passed by and offered them drinks. "Ladies, would you like a Lotus Blossom?"

A little too quickly, Karyn lifted a long-stemmed martini glass from the tray. "Yes, thank you."

She took a long drink, surprised by the strength of the drink. Warmth immediately filled her belly. When Tess glanced away, she quickly downed the remainder and exchanged her empty glass for another.

Tess turned back and Karyn smiled. "I'm sure you'll have no trouble selling that house, Tess. The location alone will move that property in no time."

"I agree," Tess said, before giving her a little hug. "And I'm sorry. I know you two were close."

"Thanks, Tess. But I'm okay. Really, I am."

"Hey, Sis!" Joie moved in next to her. "I have a little man who is dying to spend some time with his Aunt Karyn."

With a sympathetic nod, Tess patted her arm, then excused herself and headed to talk to a group in the kitchen, leaving Karyn to down her drink so she could hold Hudson.

"Wow. I can't believe I'm simply watching everyone else drink while I stay stone-cold sober," Joie lamented. "I can't believe how motherhood changes a gal." Her sister eyed the empty martini glass. "But it looks like you are holding down the fort for the both of us."

Karyn's eyes narrowed. "What do you mean?"

Joie leaned close, whispered, "That's your second, if I saw correctly."

Karyn felt her cheeks turn warm. "I—I'm just—"

Joie put her arm around Karyn's shoulder. "You don't have to explain. I get it." Her expression turned sympathetic. "Just be careful. Martinis are pure alcohol and they can sneak up on you." She looked around at the party. "I'm sure Colby is thrilled his mother invited the entire town."

Karyn lifted the sleeping baby from her sister's arms. "Well, it doesn't look like the whole town showed up."

Joie shook her head. "No, it doesn't." She sighed. "But, right now, I've got to pee. Can you watch him?"

Karyn nodded. "Sure."

She moved to the sofa, sat and focused on her nephew—on his tiny button nose, his little pink lips. No worries creased his brow as he dozed in her arms.

It wasn't long before the alcohol starting doing its trick and she felt almost as relaxed as little Hudson seemed, sleeping without a care in the world. In fact, one more cocktail, and she might not care that Grayson was in Alaska, likely sitting on a sofa by a crackling fire with his arm around Robin.

She drew in a deep breath and waved over one of the wait staff.

LEIGH ANN GRABBED her husband's arm and pulled him down the hall and into their bedroom.

"Geez, Leigh Ann. You're looking hot tonight in that white dress, but I didn't expect this." He ran his finger across the back of her shoulder.

She shut the door and whirled to face him. "Oh, give me a break. I'm not pulling you in here for sex. Did you see how many people failed to show? We are the social pariahs of Sun Valley. Mark, we're being shunned. I may as well join an Amish order and wear a prayer covering on my head." She looked toward the ceiling. "And I should probably carry a tire pump in my trunk from now on."

Mark shook his head. "You're being a little dramatic, don't you think?"

Leigh Ann's eyes filled with sudden tears. "I wanted this to be nice for Colby."

Mark took hold of her shoulders. "Honey, it is nice. The important people are all here. Besides, when I get this financial thing turned around, we both know our sunny-day friends will come crawling back. They'll want to attend our parties, because we'll be rich again and you throw the best parties of anyone I know. Now, let's get back out there and enjoy this last night with our kid, huh?"

She sniffed, feeling a lump grow inside her throat. "Yeah, you're right. This is about our son, and I'm not going to let all this other stuff mar his send-off."

She followed him out just in time to see two servers exit the kitchen carrying out the large cake she'd ordered. Vanilla crème, Colby's favorite. The top was decorated with little army tanks and toy soldiers she'd kept from his childhood.

The sight made her tear up again.

Colby saw her, smiled. He clasped his wife's hand and they waved her over.

When she reached her son's side, he wrapped his arm around her and shushed the crowd. "Hey, everyone—I just want to take a few moments to thank everyone for coming out tonight. It really means a lot to me. And I want to extend appreciation to my mom. She obviously went over and beyond on this party, the way she often does. I'm really grateful." He leaned and kissed her cheek. In response, she grabbed his hand and held it tight.

The fingers were a lot longer, the palm far sturdier when compared to the little boy hand she used to hold while crossing the street. If she could, she'd hang tightly and never let him cross into this next stage of life. She'd keep him here in Sun Valley, safe and close to her.

Colby placed his arm around his dad's shoulder. "While I'm often remiss in saying so out loud, my parents mean so much to me. I'm really going to miss you guys."

This time she could swear it was her son's eyes that turned watery with emotion.

"Anyway," he continued. "The army provides the best training available. No doubt, I'll be home soon. But until then, you can count on me giving this endeavor my all. I am proud to be a soldier in the United States Army."

A round of applause went up across the room. "Here's to Colby," someone shouted. The guests all raised their glasses. "To Colby," they chanted in unison.

"To my baby," Leigh Ann whispered.

A noise from behind caused Leigh Ann to turn.

Karyn moved forward, a martini glass wobbling in her hand. "Yup, here's to Colby," she said, splashing a good measure of Lotus Blossom on Leigh Ann's expensive carpet.

Leigh Ann and Joie exchanged worried glances. "What in the world?" Leigh Ann muttered as Joie pushed off little Hudson to Clint.

The two women moved simultaneously in their sister's direction. Their father headed that way as well, but Leigh Ann held up her hand. "We've got her, Dad."

Karyn turned her glass to Nicole. "And here's to another girl being left behind," Karyn said loudly, her words slurred. "I'm warning you, honey. The nights get awfully long when the man you love is nowhere to be found. And the worst? The worst is when you're sitting on the pot and run out of toilet paper and have no one to bring you an extra roll." She giggled. At the same time, her eyes filled with tears.

Leigh Ann apologized to her guests while she and Joie

quickly wrapped their arms around their sister and started leading her from the room. "And don't even get me started on Grayson Chandler," Karyn called back over her shoulder. "Did you all hear he's selling his house? Yup—he ain't never coming back."

6

L eigh Ann stood over Karyn with her hands parked on her hips. "So, are you going to spend the entire night on my bathroom floor wrapped around the base of the toilet?"

Damp hair was pasted against her sister's cheek, her eyes red and swollen and her face matched the gray pallor of uncooked shrimp. She pried one eye open and groaned against the light, held up an open palm. "Not now."

"Not now?" Leigh Ann challenged, keeping her voice low so as not to wake the entire household. "I need to make an appointment in order to tell you what you did was stupid? What were you thinking? A can of pork and beans has more common sense." She took a breath before launching another barrage of accusations. "Those cocktails were nearly straight vodka and people tell me you helped yourself to several. That's not you."

Her sister lifted slowly from the floor, leaned on one hand, no doubt suffering a painful hangover. "I know. I'm sorry."

Leigh Ann huffed. "I know you're hurting, but frankly, Karyn, you are the last person I ever expected would let me down last night."

From the look on her sister's face, her missile had hit the target.

"I—I really am sorry. I didn't mean to ruin the evening, especially this particular—" Karyn's words faded as she sat up. "You and I both know I rarely drink." Her eyes puddled. "I didn't do this on purpose, Leigh Ann."

Taking pity, Leigh Ann backed off a little. "I didn't mean to suggest you had. But throwing that much alcohol into your blood stream is foolish and reckless. You scared all of us half to death. I might expect that from Joie, but not you. What kind of example were you setting for your nephews?"

"Okay, now you're just getting mean."

Leigh Ann opened her mouth to argue, then thought better of it. She couldn't remember the last time she and Karyn had disagreed about anything significant, doubted they'd ever had a serious argument, let alone what could be called a fight.

They fell uncomfortably silent.

Perhaps it was best to just let the weight of her words rest on her sister a bit. "I don't have time to sit and hash this out with you, Karyn. My family will be up anytime and I want to have coffee and breakfast waiting."

Leigh Ann turned and headed down the hall and toward the kitchen, now more worried than angry.

She hadn't stopped to consider Karyn might be in trouble. After Dean died, her sister had remained in bed for weeks— barely eating or bothering to comb her hair. It'd taken a lot of pushing to get her in for some counseling, which helped. But even that had done little to pull her completely out of a funk that had lasted over two years. She never found her footing again until she met Grayson. No doubt, losing him had dealt another severe blow.

Despite being angry with Karyn for ruining the party, Leigh Ann wanted to be there for her sister this time as well, but frankly, she was puttering on low these days. What, with their financial state and Colby's leaving, she barely had enough juice to keep her own tank running.

Still, somehow she knew she would dig deep and find the resources she needed to take hold of her sister and guide her safely through this loss as well.

But not today.

Today she needed to focus on saying goodbye to her son.

KARYN LEANED AGAINST THE HARD, cold porcelain toilet with her head in her hands. Yesterday morning, she woke believing she couldn't feel much worse. She was wrong. There was another layer of despair, heightened by the fact she'd brought the situation on herself.

Leigh Ann was absolutely right. What had she been thinking?

While she didn't remember the entire evening, the snippets she could recall were humiliating.

Karyn cringed, knowing she'd have to find a way to make it up to all of them. She'd rather die than displease her family. They must be so disappointed in her.

Another wave of nausea hit. She grabbed the rim on the toilet and held her breath, waiting for the threat of retching to pass. Clearly she'd punished the lining of her stomach with far too much alcohol, and it was punching back.

One thing was for sure—she was done with all that. The numbness wasn't worth the brutal aftermath.

There were good things in her life, sure. Her family, of course. And her job at the Sun Valley Lodge. She loved living in this community and enjoying all this resort town had to offer. She had a history in this town, had grown up here. People knew her, and she knew them. She liked that.

She had many reasons to be happy. Even so, evenings and

early mornings were cruel, those hours when the silence was its loudest.

Her biggest fear? She might spend the rest of her life without a mate, without someone to love her in the way a husband loves his wife. What if she never experienced the joy of holding her own baby?

She slowly lifted from the floor, stood on unsteady feet in front of the mirror, gazing at the mascara smears under her eyes. She'd spent enough hours in front of a counselor to know she had to learn to accept what she had no power to change.

She'd survived losing Dean. Somehow she had to find a way to accept Grayson's decision and move on.

OVER THE PAST SEVERAL WEEKS, Leigh Ann pushed for traveling with Colby to the base where he'd deploy out of, even if his orders came in and she and Mark had to fly across the country. In the end, she'd lost her battle. Only Nicole would go.

"But, Mark—" she'd argued upon learning of her son's decision. "Say something to him. Tell him we want to be there too."

Her husband clasped her shoulders, looked her in the eyes. "Honey, I know this is hard. It is for me as well. But, we have no choice but to honor our son's decision."

It took every ounce of self-control not to argue. Unfortunately, as she'd learned over and over lately, her wishes weren't the ones that counted.

Leigh Ann cracked an egg into the bowl already filled with flour, oil and baking powder. She beat the batter furiously.

According to the army, her work as a mother was done. They'd even sent her and Mark a letter last week advising they could no longer claim their son on their income tax. Even though Colby was still technically a student for the greatest part of the year, he had taken the oath. He was officially emancipated. *He's in the army, now, ma'am.* Soldiers don't need their mommies.

Even if Colby hadn't snuck off and enlisted, he no longer needed her to baby him or make him pancakes or keep after him about whether he was keeping his socks clean. He had a wife now.

So, after she'd flipped the final pancake, poured the last of the coffee—she finally sat down next to her son at the kitchen table. Mark was in the shower and Nicole was still in the bedroom packing. Karyn had fallen asleep in the guest bedroom and her dad and Joie were on their way over. This might well be her final opportunity for a few minutes alone with her son, her last chance to get him to change his mind.

"Colby, I want—"

"Mom, you know why I didn't want you and Dad to come, right?" he said, cutting her off. He covered her hand with his own. "Because they say it's much harder on the family."

Leigh Ann wanted to ask just who comprised the *they* who had made that decision on her behalf. Someone wearing an army uniform hardly knew better than she what was best for their family. She opened her mouth to push the fact that they had every right to be with him, but Colby smiled a—*there-she goes-again*—kind of smile.

She nibbled the inside of her cheek to keep from tearing up. "Okay, if that's what you want. But, we'll still get to Facetime?"

He assured her they would. "And we can do some live videos in the family group Joie is setting up on Facebook."

Her heart thudded painfully against her chest. "It's not the same. And, you're going to be gone a whole year."

Colby forced a brightness on his face. "You'll be surprised at how quickly twelve months will pass."

That may be true, she thought. But he wouldn't be home for Christmas. He'd be nearly six thousand miles away eating God knows what instead of her prime rib and potato casserole, which was one of his favorites.

"What I'm doing is important, Mom."

Her fingers traced the rim of her coffee mug. "Yeah, I know it is." She ignored the sick feeling inside her stomach and drilled him with a look. "You listen to me. It's far more important that you return to us, safe and sound."

He grinned.

"No, Colby. Don't brush this notion off. I'm serious. I couldn't take it. So, don't go trying to be some hero and put yourself in a bad situation. You hear me?" She needed to find a way to make him understand that this wasn't like the times he'd lined up his plastic soldiers along the wall and knocked them all down with his hand. Or, when he engaged in combat in those awful video games he'd grown so fond of. "This isn't make-believe," she cautioned. "You are heading into a very real situation where—"

"Mom," he said. "You worry too much."

He leaned and reached in his jeans pocket, pulled out a little velvet box. "Look, I got you something."

Leigh Ann's eyes widened. "What's this?"

Her son's eyes gleamed with anticipation as he pushed the box in her direction. "Open it and find out."

She took the box, examined it.

"C'mon, open it," he urged, looking very much like the six-year-old who wrapped up his favorite rock and gave it to her for Mother's Day.

She smiled and slowly lifted the tiny hinged lid. Inside was a pendant, gold and in the shape of a heart. Her fingers caressed the engraving.

My Mom is My Hero

She lowered her eyes, turned away to keep him from seeing her eyes welling with tears. "Thank you, Son. That means a lot."

She stood then and wrapped her arms around Colby. "I love you."

He hugged her back. "I love you too, Mom."

7

"Oh my stars! Look at the darlin' baby." Madeline Crane extended her arms. "Here, give that tiny boy to me." She moved across the law firm's reception area, her four-inch stilettos sinking deep into the pale yellow carpet.

Joie grinned and passed off her tiny son to her law partner. "Even at six weeks, he's already sleeping hours at a stretch, eats well and the doctor says he is doing great."

"No doubt." Maddy leaned and kissed Hudson's soft cheek, leaving a trace of hot pink lipstick. "He has a great momma."

Quinn Ferrari peeked her head out from her office door down the hall with a wide grin. "Do I hear our baby has entered the house?" She joined them and peeked over Maddy's shoulder. "My, that little guy is growing."

"Too fast," Joie replied, shifting the weight of both the briefcase and the diaper bag on her shoulder.

It was true. In the few short weeks since Hudson made his unexpected arrival on the mountainside behind her father's sheep ranch, he'd put on several pounds and had grown two inches. While she was anxious to return to the law practice she loved, the step was another in the march of time. Admittedly, she fought a bit of melancholy over the fact her infant would be a toddler in a blink of an eye.

Margaret Adele King looked up from her post behind the reception counter. She drilled them with a stern look. "When you're all are done coo'ing over that baby, I'd like to remind you there's a client waiting in the conference room."

They'd hired Margaret Adele to replace Heather who, only after a few months, quit to become a full-time sales consultant for an internet cosmetic company. Margaret Adele hadn't been Joie's first choice. She was a bit gruff and well, focused.

Margaret Adele was an older woman with wide shoulders and no eye lids—a take no crap kind of lady. "Perhaps we need someone more—well, more inviting," Joie mentioned to Maddy after the employment interview concluded.

"I know Margaret Adele can be a little brusque, but she recently lost her husband to dementia after nursing him for years. That darlin' has no children, no family—and now very little monetary resources with retirement age looming. I'd like to give her a chance."

That's what Joie most loved about Maddy Crane—her willingness to give others an often undeserved chance. She'd been the recipient of that generosity. Maddy had invited her to become a law partner when her own life was in shambles.

Maddy passed little Hudson, who was now sound asleep, back to Joie. "Get him settled and then join us in the conference room?"

Joie nodded. "Sure thing. I'll be right in."

In her office, Joie carefully placed Hudson in his crib over by the window and adjusted the swaddle sack around his slumbering body. She clipped the baby monitor on her belt, then tested to make sure she could hear any sound her baby might make. Next, she turned on the video monitor and arranged the camera to point in the right position, then opened the app on her phone for another test.

Convinced everything was set, she gave one final look around her office, adjusted the blinds on the window overlooking Baldy Mountain and headed for the conference room.

Maddy smiled as she entered the room. "There you are! Joie, this is Jack Brannen. He's come in today to ask our help with a neighbor."

The balding man stood, revealing he was not much taller than Joie's chest. His pants were badly hemmed and nearly covered his shoes. He pushed his black-rimmed glasses up on his nose. "Yes, I have a problem that needs some legal expertise." Without looking her in the eyes, he quickly shook her hand, then sat and shuffled the stack of papers before him on the conference table. "You see, I live in a very high-end neighborhood. Well, as you know, many of the developments here in Sun Valley are upscale, but then I digress. Anyway, my neighbor built an enormous shed right by the side of his patio and painted it green. Not only do the city ordinances prohibit accessory buildings without a permit, but our homeowner's association denied his request. I know, because I am president of the HOA. Third year running. He failed to heed our pronouncements and built anyway. Laughed about it, actually." He turned to Maddy. "I want to sue this shady character for all he's got."

Maddy's eyebrows lifted, as if amused. "Well, I can certainly understand how upsetting that situation is for you. While the firm makes it a practice to never promise a certain outcome, we could certainly research the issue and report back your options and what we can do to support you legally—right, Joie?"

She nodded. "Yes, we'd be happy to look into what remedies you may have available."

Looking satisfied, Mr. Brannen adjusted his tie. "I appreciate that." He dug in the stack of papers. "In the meantime, here are photos of that horrible shed along with copies of the covenants for our neighborhood and the ordinances the city officials told me were relevant." He slid the material across the desk. "The city council meeting is at seven o'clock tonight."

"Tonight?" Joie exchanged glances with Maddy.

"Mr. Brannen, I'm afraid the short time frame won't be to our advantage," Maddy cautioned. "Without more time, we may not be able to prepare adequately. Unfortunately, I also have a scheduling conflict this evening—a prior commitment that can't be rearranged. And Joie, well—she has commitments as well."

He reached across and grasped Joie's hand, his eyes imploring. "The shed—did I tell you it's green?"

Maddy shook her head. "I wish we could do more for you, Mr. Brannen. We can still pursue the matter, even if tonight's meeting is off the table."

Joie took a deep breath and cut in. "I'll attend," she said confidently. "Quinn can help me prepare and I'll appear at the hearing —do what I can."

Maddy looked skeptical. "Are you sure, sweet thing? I mean, this is your first day back and you have—well, like I said, you have other commitments."

Joie ignored the yellow light going off inside her head, the one that hinted she was being impulsive. "No, I can handle it." She wanted to assure herself, more than anyone, that she was no less a lawyer because motherhood had been added to her résumé. "The hearing won't take much more than an hour."

Maddy stirred her tea thoughtfully. "Well, if you think you can, I'm sure Mr. Brannen would appreciate it."

"Oh, I do," he assured them with a slightly crooked grin. "I'm tired of being ignored. Let's kick some a—." He hesitated. "Let's trounce this guy."

"I'll do my best," Joie promised. "But remember, we are appearing before the city council, not a judge. We're a long way from bringing a lawsuit. What we're going for tonight is a decision that forces your neighbor to remove the shed."

"The *green* shed," their new client reminded.

"Yes, the green shed."

Back in her office, Joie placed a call to Leigh Ann to see if she could babysit little Hudson only to learn Leigh Ann and Mark were traveling to Boise.

"Colby relented and is letting us accompany them as far as Boise. We'll say our goodbyes at the airport," she explained. "I wish I could help you out. Maybe Karyn is free."

She struck out there too. Karyn had an appointment to get her hair highlighted. "I can re-schedule," she offered. While she'd like to take her up on the offer, Joie was reluctant to take advantage, even if her sister was willing to forfeit her appointment with the new stylist. Besides, Leigh Ann told her Karyn had spent the night on her bathroom floor. No doubt, she'd want to turn in early and there was no telling how late this meeting might run.

Next on the list was her dad. Unfortunately, he was attending a grazing meeting.

In the end, she had no choice but to call Clint.

"I'm sorry. I'm really in a spot," she explained on the phone. "I promise I won't be gone over a couple of hours. If I feed him just before I leave, he'll likely sleep the entire time."

"Sure, I'll watch him," he told her. "I'll head that way right after I finish up at the stables."

Relief flooded through her. "Thanks, Clint. I knew I could count on you."

What she didn't count on was how it would feel to walk out the door and leave little Hudson behind. She fought tears all the way to the car, realizing she'd always been with those perfect little newborn eyelashes and impossibly tiny fingernails, his dimpled hands and small toes. For months, Hudson had never been further away than her own heartbeat. Now, she was putting miles between them.

Despite fighting the urge to turn around and go back, Joie pulled into the parking lot at City Hall promptly at six o'clock, determined to trade her mommy hat for a lawyer cap—at least for a little while.

The room where the city council met was fairly nondescript. The walls were painted a neutral beige. The dais up front where the council members sat was made of wood. Rows of chairs filled the remainder of the room, except for a small table at the back with coffee and tea.

Joie took her seat next to Jack Brannen. Across the aisle sat a man with a precise haircut and a stiffly pressed white button-down shirt, rolled at the sleeves just high enough to reveal what appeared to be a Jaeger-LeCoultre watch—a time piece she knew had cost well over ten grand. She'd seen one featured in an article in a magazine at the doctor's office while taking Hudson in for a well-baby check.

Mr. Brannen leaned her way. "That's him, my neighbor. Reeve Rusk."

"*The* Reeve Rusk?" Joe whispered, incredulously. "The property records listed a corporation."

"One of many he hides behind, no doubt." The diminutive man scratched at his bald head. "Doesn't matter how rich he is— he can't build a green shed next to my house."

Joie kicked herself for not doing her homework. She hated surprises. Especially when the surprise was a business magnate who just so happened to land on the list of the ten wealthiest men in America several years in a row. His entrepreneurial career included starting a web-based software company that sold for millions. He went on to found a highly successful energy company and two non-profit research companies, one of which was on the cutting edge in the field of brain neuroscience.

While that was enough to get him on the front covers of many top magazines, there also seemed to be an obsession with his personal life. He was ruggedly handsome, had remained single and rarely dated, and traveled around the world at whim in a yacht that was larger than many elementary schools.

That he'd bought property in Sun Valley and had successfully kept the fact out of the news was a feat. Of course, this hearing would change all that, not to overshadow the noteworthy fact he'd shown up personally to address such a minor matter.

Jack Brannen's petition was the first up on the agenda. The clerk read the proposition into the record, barely able to tear her eyes from the celebrity in the audience.

Before Joie could stand to address the council, Reeve Rusk rose from his seat. "Excuse me, I may be out of order here, but I'd like to simply clear this issue up by offering to remove the shed."

Joie blinked. "I'm sorry?" She also stood. "You want to take the shed down? And we had to come all the way to a city council meeting for you to decide that?"

A tense hush blanketed the meeting room.

"Why not just take the shed down when my client asked you to? Or, when the HOA sent their multiple letters?" She felt herself getting more steamed than the issue likely warranted. Still, she hated when wealth was equated with privilege. She turned to the council. "While Mr. Rusk's offer to remove the shed is certainly accepted, I hope his arrogance will be duly noted in the record."

Next to her, Jack Brannen clasped his pudgy fingers together with pure satisfaction written all over his face.

Mr. Rusk cleared his throat. "This lady is correct. I behaved horribly and have taken up the time of this council and that of my neighbor and his attorney. While I'm afraid it was some of my people and not me personally who ignored the situation, I will personally make restitution for the residual effect." He turned to a man Joie just now noticed—a guy who sat behind Mr. Rusk wearing a tailored suit. "Stan, please write the City of Sun Valley a check for enough to cover,"—he paused and scanned the agenda in his hand, then pointed to an item on the paper—"this library addition." He smiled over at her client. "And a check in a matching amount to Mr. Brannen."

Now Jack Brannen's eyes were filled with absolute glee. "That's very generous. Thank you," he said.

"Yes, very generous," remarked one of the councilmen sitting on the dais.

Joie wasn't so sure the gesture was magnanimous, or merely some superior grandstanding. Either way, her client was happy. That's what mattered.

Without acknowledging the man's gesture, she turned to Mr. Brannen. "I'm glad things turned out to your satisfaction," she told him, while gathering her files.

He thanked her just as her cell phone buzzed in her purse. She scrambled to retrieve the phone from her bag and saw that it was Clint.

"Look, I've got to go." She patted Mr. Brannen on the arm and headed from the meeting room, pulled the phone to her ear. "Clint? Is everything all right?"

"Yeah, don't get worried. Hudson's fine. I just needed you to know there's a report of a fire over at Leigh Ann's house."

8

"Who would do such a thing?" Leigh Ann surveyed her prize rose garden, now ruined. "I had that Bathsheba variety shipped from England. And my Lady Emma Hamilton fragranced the entire yard. All of my roses are gone," she wailed.

Karyn wrapped an arm around her sister's shoulder. "I'll help you plant them again."

Joie turned to Rory Sparks, the town sheriff. "Do we have any clues as to who set fire to my sister's rose garden?"

He shook his head. "Unfortunately, not yet. We do know the fire was not an accident." He pointed to a pile of smoldering embers. "Someone intentionally piled up wood and set it on fire."

Mark frowned and marched nervously in a circle. "It could have burnt our entire house down." He shook his head. "No doubt this prank has to do with the Preston, USA deal."

Rory fingered his chin. "Uh, could be. But we shouldn't jump to conclusions."

"What other conclusion makes sense?" Mark challenged. "Give me another good reason why someone would torch my wife's roses, if not to get back at me?"

Leigh Ann nodded in agreement. "Yes, and someone flattened the tires on my car earlier this week."

Mark jabbed the air with his finger in sheriff's direction. "I know what I know. Both of these incidents were on purpose."

Rory pulled out a tiny spiral notebook from his front pocket and a pen. "Well, yes—I'd have to agree that two incidents of this nature seem a bit suspicious. Let's just take down some details."

Joie and Karyn flanked Leigh Ann and led her inside. "C'mon, they'll take it from here. Let's get you some tea, huh?"

Leigh Ann shook her head. "And we missed Colby's send off at the Boise airport."

Inside, Leigh Ann curled up on the sofa and draped the afghan over her lap. "You don't suppose whoever did this might do something worse?"

Joie quickly shook her head. "No, I doubt it. The culprit wanted to make a point and accomplished that. It's highly unlikely someone would risk getting caught by taking this whole prank thing any further. Especially now that there's a police report on file."

Karyn agreed. "You shouldn't worry," she said, but her face betrayed her words.

Mark had stronger words to say when he came in. "These cowards need to take their anger out on me, not you," he told her, rubbing her shoulders. "I'm sorry, Leigh Ann. I never expected this is how everything would turn out. It's bad enough I put our finances in jeopardy."

She reached and squeezed one of his hands. "People make mistakes." She sought his face, wanting desperately to raise his spirits. "We can't turn back the clock and have a re-do. We would if we could, but we can't. The only option we have now is to move forward. People need to let us do that."

Perhaps that little talk was more for her than anyone else. If she allowed her mind to follow its natural path, she'd be in a heap on the bedroom carpet. Daily, she had to force herself to look their friends and neighbors in the eyes, knowing what they must think.

It'd been humiliating having their credit card turned down. While she hadn't dwelt on the fact, their cash resources were very limited and dwindling quickly. Mark needed to get something figured out, and fast. While she was good at faking a bright smile, there was only so much more she could emotionally take.

Despite being head-over-heels in love with each other in the early years of their marriage, they'd had their share of problems when Mark took crazy risks with their finances.

Once, back when Colby was a baby, Mark depleted their meager checking account and invested in multi-tiered company that sold plastic kitchenware. "It's the next Tupperware, honey," he'd assured her. She refrained from reminding him Tupperware took a hit when Walmart mass-stocked their shelves with a competitor product.

Next came a pet company with a splashy ad campaign and a mascot that looked like a sock puppet. Unfortunately, a potential customer base of millions of pet owners just wasn't enough. Even fifty million in investment capital couldn't keep the company afloat, with much of the problem traced back to a business plan that included selling items below cost. Mark borrowed thousands to invest, and they'd lost it all.

It wasn't until Mark hit upon his knack for real estate that things turned around and he made any real money. Not only had he invested in some well-placed real estate investment stocks, but he flipped some properties here in the Sun Valley area and made significant profit. They'd lived with few financial worries for many years—until he'd recently parlayed their riches in a scheme to take over Preston, USA. When the company fought back, their personal balance sheet took a dive that rivaled jumping head first into an empty pool. If Mark didn't secure some income soon, there would be much more to worry about than flat tires and burnt rose bushes.

No matter how much she loved her husband and wanted to support his ego, she knew she might have to take matters into her own hands if she wanted this situation turned around quickly.

Days later, she found herself revisiting this notion when she came home from a jog with Karyn to find Mark lounging on the sofa with the television remote in hand, wearing nothing but his t-shirt and underwear. His hair was a wild mess and he hadn't shaved in days.

"Mark, what are you doing home?" she asked, her heart sinking. "I thought you were meeting some investors for lunch today."

"They cancelled," he said, not bothering to pull his eyes from the television. "You know, that Ina Garten can cook circles around any of the rest of them, Paula Deen included. And I like her sense of style." He looked over at her, smiled. "She reminds me a lot of you, honey."

Despite the compliment, she had to bite her tongue to keep from snarling out loud. "What does that mean, that they canceled? Did they reschedule?"

Mark tossed the remote onto the sofa table. "No."

Leigh Ann parked her hands on her hips. "Mark, this isn't like you, lying around all day, watching daytime television and eating chocolates." She pointed to the empty candy box on the table. "You're acting like I did when I was six months pregnant."

"Excuse me, you were hitting people."

Leigh Ann rolled her eyes. "Only two, and the mailman had the good taste never to bring that up again."

Mark failed to laugh. "You said you wanted to support me."

"My mistake. I assumed you'd have a dream worth supporting. I have no intention of encouraging more of your sofa loafing."

"Leigh Ann, stop it! Get off my back, will you? I have enough pressure without you nagging me day and night."

Her eyes immediately filled with angry tears. Her mouth was honed sharp as any pair of kitchen shears. If she had a mind to, she could slice him to shreds. She also knew that sometimes there was more power in restraint. So instead, she gave him a piercing look, turned and silently walked into the kitchen.

It wasn't that she didn't want to give him the benefit of the doubt, or to be supportive. But this recent pattern scared her to death. Mark had simply quit trying. It was as if he'd given up.

Abdicating was not an option. Not when so much was at stake.

Mark had maneuvered this bus into the ditch, but with a little work and cunning planning, she'd climb into the driver's seat and get them back out on the highway—at least until he rallied and took over the wheel.

Leigh Ann lifted her chin with renewed determination.

For several years, she'd single handedly managed this town's events in her volunteer position with the tourism council, including the Trailing of the Sheep Festival each fall—five days of nonstop family events including multicultural performers, culinary events, a Sheepherders' Ball and the big Sheep Parade with fifteen hundred sheep trailing down Main Street.

Last year, the combined attendance at the five-day festival topped twenty-five thousand, coming from thirty-six states and twenty-two foreign countries. The economic impact was estimated to be at over four million.

She had a lot of markers she could call in, and she intended to do just that at the planning meeting tonight.

If Mark had investors lined up, he could find a way forward. Perhaps he and Andrea DePont could quickly locate another potential target company, one that needed infused funding. Equity Capital could step in and become the hero this time. She could help that happen.

Power dressing in this day and age had less to do with style than substance. She needed an outfit that said she was a no-nonsense woman—someone who demanded respect, which is why she shuffled in her closet until her hands landed on an outfit by an Italian designer she adored, an ensemble consisting of a classic gray skirt and a short-waist jacket in the same color that had cost far more than she'd ever admit to anyone. She paired the pieces with a light apricot silk blouse, to soften the look a bit. Her shoes would complete the attire—a pair of patent leather Christian Louboutin's in black.

Satisfied she looked ready to take on the world—or in this case, the business leaders of Sun Valley—she grabbed her bag and headed to the car.

The tourism office was located on the corner of Sun Valley Road and East Avenue in the upper floor of a former bank building that now housed a coffee shop. Despite the convenience, Leigh Ann much preferred to grab her morning mocha latte at Bistro on Fourth, if nothing more than to support her good friend, Nash Billingsley. Even so, the girls behind the counter were friends and she waved as she passed by, stopping at the rack of travel materials to straighten some brochures featuring the many bike trails in the area, then headed for the stairs.

At the top, she turned and moved for the door to the conference room.

"Good morning, everyone," she said, greeting the men and women gathered around the table.

There was Betty Lionel, a CPA and huge supporter of the tourism initiatives they'd put in place. Les Rickart and Marsden Winder owned one of the most successful property management outfits in town. Mark had helped make them a lot of money.

At the end of the table sat the Dilworth sisters. Trudy and Ruby attended every meeting without exception. There were others, many she'd known for years, including Leo Gabbert, the Chamber of Commerce director.

"We have a fairly packed agenda to discuss," she told them, passing out printed copies. "But before we do, I have something I need to visit with you about. A personal matter."

Leigh Ann sat in her chair at the head of the table, leaned

over the granite surface and steepled her fingers. "As you know, my husband Mark has contributed to this community in a number of ways over all the years we've been married, which is far more than I care to count."

Nervous laughter went up from around the table.

"And, while Mark's recent business venture was a bit miscalculated, over the years he never ceased to support the financial viability of the Sun Valley area and our businesses—*your* businesses." She directed her attention to the woman sitting at the other end of the table. "Betty, do you remember when you first passed the exam and hung your shingle? Mark and I hosted a dinner party and you signed up enough clients that evening to keep you going through the first tax season. Marsden, same with you. Mark has thrown a lot of business your way, given plenty of word-of-mouth recommendations whenever possible."

She held up her wrist, which sported a beautiful bracelet. "Miss Trudy, remember when you asked me to purchase some of Lindsay's work? You said your new protégé needed some sales to build her confidence and I got out my checkbook without question."

Leigh Ann perused the room, noted many of their eyes were directed at the table. "Well, as difficult as it is to ask—"

Leo, the Chamber of Commerce director, held up two open palms. "Leigh Ann, stop. We have something we need to address before you go any further." He stood, wearing a solemn expression. "I'm afraid we've been inundated with complaints."

Betty pulled a stack of envelopes from her briefcase and held them up. "A lot of complaints. There's far more on our email server."

The muscle in her neck tightened. "What kind of complaints?"

Leo shook his head slowly. "A lot of people were hurt financially when Mark and that woman from San Francisco tried to take over Preston, USA. Emotions are running high in the aftermath. I'm afraid many in the community are asking for you to be relieved of your duties here on the tourism council."

"They want me gone?" She swallowed. "I'm a volunteer. You can't fire me!"

Miss Trudy looked like she was about to cry. Ruby too.

"Are you all in agreement with this?" she challenged, looking around the table.

"Not all of us," Miss Trudy told her. "Me and Ruby—well, we don't agree with this decision." The ample-bosomed woman glanced angrily at the rest of them. "I think we should just wait it out, let these hot emotions blow over."

Leo rubbed at his temples. "I don't like it either, but we rely heavily on the contributions of our patrons." He held up the stack. "Unfortunately, our donors have spoken—loudly."

Leigh Ann's back stiffened. "I see. So, you just want me to bow out gracefully—not cause any trouble." She posed it not as a question, but a statement.

They all nodded weakly, then dropped their collective gaze at the table again.

"Fine," she told them, her heart pounding. "I'll go."

Miss Trudy looked up, eyes brimming with emotion. "Like I said, this will blow over. I'll be the first to champion your return when it does," she promised.

"Thank you, Miss Trudy."

Leigh Ann's hands trembled as she scooped up her pen and returned it to her purse. She stood, straightened her expensive gray jacket, then turned and walked out.

Outside, she climbed in her car, determined to keep her expression stoic. She never knew who might be watching.

Event planning is more than putting on a party. A skilled planner knows how to minimize problems. After you've organized half a dozen events, you realize that you don't have to invent the form each time. Some things universally work, and some don't. You must send invitations by mail, important people must feel pampered. Nobody eats crudités unless the vegetables are fancy. Speeches should never last more than seven minutes.

Not anyone off the street would know this.

Leigh Ann started the car and wove her way out of the parking lot, trying not to think about what had just transpired. At the light, she waited for traffic to clear before turning right onto Main Street. She'd only traveled a few yards before she realized she'd gone the wrong direction.

Her grip tightened to a near death grip on the steering wheel.

She maneuvered a quick u-turn and headed to Hamilton's Nursery for a quick stop. Minutes later, she loaded her car with several flats of vegetables.

In all the many years she'd served as director of the tourism council, she'd never missed a deadline, never botched an event. Never once had she let this town down.

Now, they wanted her gone?

Let them try to find someone to fill her shoes, someone who could pull off the myriad of tasks better than she had.

She climbed back in the car and headed south. As she turned off the main highway to the road leading to the ranch, the view turned to vigorous stands of aspens and willows lining the east fork of the Big Wood, the meadow grasses tall and dotted with wildflowers and occasional sagebrush.

She passed under a familiar large hand-carved wooden ranch sign that read *ABBOTT RANCH* and drove into the graveled yard surrounded by buildings, all made of rough-hewn logs.

To the right was the cookhouse. Past that, the barn and the bunkhouse, the riding arena and the small guesthouse where Joie had lived before moving into town. Up the canyon, she could see the lambing sheds and the corrals in the distance.

The main house was on the left, an inviting log structure with an expansive lawn surrounding the building and a wrap-around porch complete with a railing and rocking chairs. Tall windows lined both the front and back provided an unobstructed view of the stunning mountainous landscape with large white cumulous clouds peeking over the pine stands. A river rock fireplace jutted from the southern end. Nearby, a wood shed filled to the brim promised warm fires to come.

Leigh Ann climbed from her car, bent and greeted her dad's border collie. "Hey, Riley. How are you, girl?" She patted the dog's head with one hand, while opening the rear door of her SUV.

Her father's pickup was nowhere in sight. She remembered, then, that he and Sebastian had driven to Twin Falls to pick up a new stock trailer. Disappointed, she pulled the first of many flats of vegetable starts from her vehicle—tomatoes and pea plants, watermelon vines and the beginnings of what would become tall corn stalks. In the past, she'd planted from seed, but no longer. That was one of a long list of changes in her life.

Her dad's dog wagged its tail wildly and circled her ankles. "What's the matter, girl? You got left home?" She wedged the flat against her hip and slammed the door shut with her free hand. "Well, come on. You can hang with me."

Leigh Ann walked across the packed gravel yard, past the path leading to the main house and headed for the barn where she set the flats on the ground. It took more than a little effort, and breaking a manicured nail, to open the massive sliding door that was known for sticking on the rail.

Inside, sunlight shown through several glass windows and provided just enough light for her to find exactly what she was looking for. She grabbed the shovel, turned and marched back outside, grabbed the flats and headed for an area behind the barn where she found the piece of equipment she needed.

It'd been a long while since she'd run a rototiller. She could only hope the blasted thing had gasoline in it. Setting her foot against the small tire, she turned the key and pulled the crank. After a couple of disconcerting chugs, the engine roared to life, filling the warm air with a loud noise that would chase away even the cheeriest birds.

Just as well, she thought, as she wheeled the machine into place and released the lever. The sharp prongs dug into the earth, hard from winter. Leigh Ann gripped the handles and hung on, feeling the deep vibrations in her arms as she steered the rototiller forward. Up and down the rows, she tilled the dirt, making it ready for planting.

If Mark were here, he'd argue she was wasting her time. "You can buy vegetables at Atkinson's Market much cheaper, and without all the trouble," he'd point out.

It didn't matter. There was something soothing about setting the plants, watering them. She knew that if she cultivated the plants properly, they would produce a good crop.

Not everything in life could be counted on to yield the same.

Leigh Ann worked with single-minded ardor, until every joint in her body ached. She straightened and rubbed at the small of her back, unsure exactly how much time had passed before she heard a truck pull into the yard.

Voices in the distance confirmed that her father and Sebastian had returned. She briefly considered waving, but she was almost finished. Determined, she kept at it—yanking one of the final fledgling plants from the black plastic tray and wedging it into its place in the dirt.

She pulled her hands across the surrounding soil and slammed the dirt around the little tomato plant—a beefsteak variety.

"Leigh Ann, honey?"

Her father's frame blocked the sun, creating a shadow that fell across her shoulder. Without looking up, she reached for another plant. "Yeah?" she answered, her lip quivering.

"You okay?"

She nodded and jabbed the plant into the ground. "Uh-hmm."

Her hair was now in a disheveled bun, her cheek smeared with dried dirt.

To her father's credit, he didn't mention any of this. Instead he waited several minutes before he simply laid a hand on her shoulder. "Sweetheart?"

"Yeah?"

"You do know you're wearing a business suit and heels, right?" he said.

She stopped packing dirt around the tomato plant, sat back on her haunches and looked at the hem of her expensive skirt, now black with mud—and what looked sadly like a smashed spider.

She ran a finger across the fabric, looked up at him. "Yes, I know."

Her father slowly nodded, took in her tear-stained face. "All right, honey." He gave her shoulder a squeeze, then tilted his head in the direction of the house. "I bought some dinner in town. When you're finished here, come up to the house and eat."

9

The past weeks could best be defined as a messy scramble. Joie had no idea juggling a career and motherhood would be this difficult.

She hated to admit it, but bringing little Hudson to the office hadn't worked as reliably as she'd hoped. He cried when she was on important phone calls, burped up milk all down her shoulder just before a hearing, and had a blow-out diaper that had everyone peeking their heads from their offices and asking, "What's that smell?"

Yesterday, she fell asleep while sitting straight up in a chair at the conference room table—during a client meeting!

While Maddy had been very understanding, there was a limit Joie could allow. She needed back-up childcare—someone who could drop everything and be there to cover when necessary—and she needed someone quick, like yesterday.

So, she told Margaret Adele to clear her morning calendar and she lined up interviews by placing a notice that she was looking for someone on the online community forum. That turned out to be her first big mistake.

Everybody and their dog knew someone who would be perfect for the job.

Nash Billingsley had a niece visiting for the summer, but Joie figured the skull and crossbones tattoo on her cheek might scare the baby. Heavens—it scared her!

Tess McCreary recommended a woman who had just bought a house from her, a transplant from Germantown, Ohio. But when Joie met the large square-shouldered woman, she seemed like a drill sergeant. "We keep baby on strict schedule—no? Babies require disciplined approach. Must keep the upper hand."

She'd quickly passed.

Hoping the third time might be the charm, she sat down to have lunch with a woman who finally seemed just right. Her name was Sally and she had a little girl of her own who was two-years old.

Sally was knowledgeable, personable and had a great sense of humor. "Just wait until your little one starts repeating everything he hears," she warned. "Last week, my little sweetie told her Sunday School teacher the story about Jonah and the whale was *fake news*. I finally had to turn the television off."

Sally seemed experienced. The upside was she was available immediately, so Joie hired her.

Unfortunately, the upside quickly slid into a downside when Joie discovered Sally's little sweetie also had a penchant for biting. "I'm so, so sorry," Sally apologized. "I think Tiffany was trying to satisfy her need to express difficult emotions. I'll work to help her opt for a better choice next time."

Joie fought to keep from telling the woman a swift pop to the toddler's bottom might be the best deterrent. Regardless, she wasn't willing to risk another set of tooth marks on little Hudson's arm. "I'm sorry, this just isn't going to work out," she admitted, as she wrote out a final check.

Karyn suggested what was to her the obvious. "You know Leigh Ann would help you out. She's a bit at odds with all her free time now that she isn't spending all her energy over at the tourism office. From my perspective, it's a win/win for both of you."

"Yeah, that's what I need. My big sister hovering over every parenting decision I make, reminding me daily how each and every choice affects the child I am raising to be a responsible adult." Joie shuddered. "I already deal with enough guilt, thank you."

In the end, she had no option.

"Look, Leigh Ann—this is only temporary until I can find someone. And let's be clear, I am still the mother and will make the decisions. Oh, and I intend on paying you, same as anyone else. No arguments on that. So, are we on the same page?"

Her older sister bobbed her head enthusiastically. "Of course," she promised.

So, despite Joie's reservations, on the following Monday morning she packed up little Hudson, drove over and reluctantly handed him off to Leigh Ann before heading to work.

"I've left a list of instructions inside his bag. And don't hesitate to call me if you need anything. I'll have my cell with me at all times."

"He'll be just fine," Leigh Ann promised, waving her out the door.

"Yeah, we got this," Colby's wife added from the doorway leading to the kitchen. Her face was plastered with a homemade concoction of avocados blended with buttermilk and cucumbers.

Leigh Ann tried not to roll her eyes. "Absolutely. We have it handled. Now, scoot."

Nicole leaned over Leigh Ann's shoulder and caressed the baby's cheek. "Yeah, we're going to have a party, aren't we little buddy?"

Joie gave a weak smile and reluctantly moved for the car, knowing it would be hours before she'd hold her sweet little guy in her arms.

Halfway to the curb, she turned. "Don't forget to warm his milk to—"

Both Leigh Ann and Nicole waved her on. "Go, he'll be fine."

LEIGH ANN PASSED Hudson over to Nicole and slowly slid the front door closed.

So, it had come to this. She was now a full-time babysitter. She adored her little nephew, but no one knew she'd stepped up to the plate, in part, because she needed some income, even if it was minimal.

This morning, she'd gotten up well before dawn, unable to sleep after her tense conversation with Mark the evening before.

"Mark, I am down to only a few hundred dollars in my household account. I need you to make a transfer."

He hadn't answered. Instead, he simply channel surfed until he landed on a television documentary about fishing in Alaska. "You know," he commented. "I wonder if that guy Karyn dated would ever consider taking me fishing."

"You mean Grayson? Mark, they broke up."

Her husband scratched his days-old chin stubble. "Yeah, but he still might take me fishing. I mean, he was a pretty nice guy."

Leigh Ann rolled her eyes. "That would be so inappropriate."

He looked at her like she had minnows growing from her ears, shrugged and turned the volume up on the television.

She took a deep breath, reached for the remote and muted the sound. "Mark, pay attention. Did you hear me when I said I need money transferred?"

"I heard you," he said, still not looking at her.

"So, you'll do that—transfer some money tomorrow?"

Mark sat, looked at her. "I can't. There isn't any."

She scowled. "There isn't any? What do you mean?"

"I mean, we have enough to make the house payment and

utilities for the next couple of months, but I'm not able to transfer any funds into your play account."

"My household account," she corrected, her heart now pounding. "And how am I going to buy groceries, or pay Isla?"

"Yeah, about that—"

Her eyes widened. "There's no money to pay our housekeeper?"

He stared at the floor. "Nope. Or your nails. Your pedicures. All those plants you buy at the nursery. We have no funds to go golfing, to throw any of those fancy parties, and after next week, we're down to one car. I can't make both lease payments."

Leigh Ann stared at him, stunned and trying to breathe. "But, we have money. I mean, we have cash besides what you committed in the business deal."

Her husband didn't move.

"Mark, you're scaring me."

He looked up, eyes puddled. "Yeah, you should be. Because I am."

Leigh Ann's ears started to ring with rising panic. "What are you going to do?" she asked, so shrill she didn't recognize her own voice.

"I'm trying to get this turned around," he told her. "But it's going to take time. My investment grade is in the toilet right now. Word spreads fast in the financial market. No one wants to talk to me."

"What about our real estate holdings?"

"All pledged." He stood, took her hands. "Leigh Ann, listen. The next months are going to be very tight."

She got mad then—pulled her hands from his. All of a sudden, it was as if someone entered her body and took over her mouth. "How could you let this happen? I trusted you to take care of us. You and that Andrea woman—look what you've done!"

Last year, she'd mistakenly thought he was having an affair with her. But this—well, in some ways, this was worse.

Mark's hands dropped to his sides, his eyes clouded with shame. He turned and walked to the cabinet where they kept their liquor and poured himself a healthy glass of scotch, downed it in one swallow. Then, he turned, "Leigh Ann, I'm only going to say this one last time—back off."

She mulled the entire conversation over in her mind throughout the night, tossing and turning and wondering what they were going to do.

She'd wanted to quiz him, demand he tell her his plan. They had to have a plan if they were going to weather this financial downturn.

He needed to make a list and prioritize his action items. Keep careful record of every conversation, and follow up appropriately. He needed to rally every resource, especially people for whom he'd helped increase investment portfolios in the past.

Was Mark even doing any of this? He certainly couldn't just sit around in jogging shorts and a t-shirt and watch cooking shows.

She thought of Nicole and wondered if she'd clued in to their financial fiasco?

Which was worse—having their finances zipped tight, or having anyone know that after all these years, they were on the brink of losing it all? Especially her new daughter-in-law. If she knew, she'd relay the information to Colby. Her son had enough to worry about right now without concerning himself with this mess.

Something inside her surged. Maybe it was anger, perhaps fear. Did it even matter? The important thing is that she couldn't sit around and simply do nothing while waiting for Mark to pull himself together and make something happen.

Leigh Ann slumped into an arm chair, needing to think. From the other room, she could hear Nicole singing to Hudson. At least for now, there would be some income from babysitting, even if minimal. Normally, she would argue to the hilt, absolutely refuse any sort of payment from her sister. Thankfully, Joie had made a fuss about paying her. She could just give in and accept the payment and it wouldn't raise any suspicions.

She made a note to talk to Mark, make sure he understood Nicole and Colby were never to discover what they were facing. Likewise, neither of her sisters were to know—or her dad. They might all try to help. Frankly, she'd rather die than face the shame of taking money from her family.

Next, she'd get on the internet, make an effort to track down some possibilities and do some research of her own. Everyone knew there were answers to everything on the internet.

10

"I'm sorry, Isla. I realize this is unexpected, but Mark and I need to tighten a bit." The words felt like a lump of mud in her throat. Tightening was an understatement, but for now, that's all she was willing to admit. Even then, this certainly didn't look good.

"As you know, we have Colby's wife living with us now, and we've both decided she needs some responsibility for the household while staying here."

Another partial truth.

Nicole wasn't a bit reluctant to climb in and help, but Leigh Ann was not entirely ready to acquiesce to cleaning her toilets with baking soda and white vinegar—one of Nicole's many concoctions meant to eliminate harsh chemicals she claimed were contributing to the rise in cancer in America.

In fact, her daughter-in-law had even started a blog called *The Crunchy Homestead* which featured her "clean living" lifestyle, peppered with generous doses of birthing articles, which included photographs that made Leigh Ann cringe. Some things were just better left private.

Leigh Ann looked Isla in the eyes, trying not to get emotional.

"You've been a wonderful housekeeper, Isla. I'd be happy to provide a great reference." She stopped short of offering to help secure some employment with one of her friends. She couldn't risk inviting too many questions.

"I understand," Isla told her in broken English. Something in her eyes betrayed the statement. She didn't totally understand. How could she?

For over ten years, Isla showed up to work promptly at seven every morning. She did the laundry, made beds, cleaned cupboards and drawers, dusted blinds and kept the entire house in order—just the way Leigh Ann liked.

And now she was being let go? Leigh Ann felt like an absolute heel, but she had no choice.

Of course, firing Isla was only the beginning.

She also had to find a way to explain why she was backing out of her ladies' golf league. "I'm just so busy these days. This is my attempt to whittle some things off my plate," she'd explained. The way the women looked back at her suggested they didn't buy her feeble attempt to save face. Likely, they had heard about how she was no longer helping out at the tourism council. If anything, she had more time on her hands.

Even with all this humiliation heaped on her head, the worst by far was how her relationship with Mark was disintegrating.

She was furious with him, and despite her attempts to hide the fact, she could barely be civil. Especially when he continued to lie around the house and do nothing to change their situation.

"Mark, you are never going to increase the balance of our checkbook by watching Grey's Anatomy!" she'd scolded from the doorway into the kitchen, taking advantage of the rare privacy afforded when Nicole left the house. Her raised voice scared little Hudson and sent him wailing.

"Neither is terrorizing your nephew," Mark called back over his shoulder. "Leigh Ann, I told you over and over. This crap from you—it isn't helping." He got up from the sofa and stomped into the bedroom. Minutes later, he returned wearing a pair of jogging shorts and a t-shirt. He walked straight past her and headed for the garage, slamming the door behind him.

There was no reasoning with him. He'd been in an especially bad mood after selling his motorcycle yesterday.

She supposed their financial tumble was equally as hard on him as it was for her. Even so, Leigh Ann wasn't the type to sit around and wait for something to happen to change her circumstances. Despite the fact her initial plan had failed and she'd been rebuffed by all those who she'd counted on to help, she still had to do something to keep them afloat.

She needed a job that brought in some interim income, maybe something she could do from home. Nicole seemed to be successful bringing in advertising revenue with her blog. Perhaps she could do something similar. That way she could continue to care for little Hudson, and still add to their bottom line.

Whatever money she made wouldn't completely solve the problem, of course. Turning their financial situation around was on Mark's shoulders, whether he liked it or not.

She could barely remember a time she'd been this mad at him—or this scared.

What he needed was a good slap alongside his head! Or perhaps she should take hold of one of his ears, lift him off that couch, march him into his office and demand he get to work fixing this.

Her thoughts trailed off, thinking about his ears, the sweet curl of them. He had little-boy ears, she'd thought more than once. Despite having grayed a bit at the temples, his ears were as tender as they'd been when she met him, as sweet as they must've been when he'd been a boy. She loved his ears. Then it dawned on her—how could she remain angry at him, when she felt so tenderly toward his body parts?

He needed her help, that's all. If Mark wouldn't make a task list, she would.

After placing Hudson down for his morning nap in the temporary nursery, she marched into her husband's office and yanked on his top desk drawer.

Nothing.

She jiggled the drawer—pulled harder.

Again, the drawer wouldn't budge.

Leigh Ann parked her hands on her hips. *Really, Mark? You locked the drawer?*

She huffed and rifled her fingers in the little ceramic container on his credenza. When her fingers lit on the tiny key hidden there, she pulled it out and inserted it into the tiny slot on the front of the drawer and twisted.

Voila! The drawer opened.

Leigh Ann tucked the hidden key back in place and pulled the drawer open, shifted some papers aside hoping to find an extra pad of paper. That's when she saw what Mark had been hiding.

Bankruptcy papers.

She raked the documents from the drawer and scanned the contents. Beyond the petition, there was a complete listing of assets and liabilities—in agonizing detail.

Horrified, she turned and marched through the house, papers in hand. She flung the door leading to the garage open and moved to where Mark was bent over at his tool chest, his back to her.

"When were you going to tell me?" she demanded, waving the papers in the air. "I mean, if you intend to publicize our situation to the entire world by filing all this with the court, you might want to let me in on the fact!"

Mark stopped digging through his tools, but failed to turn and look at her.

She took that as a sign of concession, and continued—her anger building. "It's not bad enough you pledged everything we own and never once thought to see what I thought about it. It's not bad enough that the lady at the checkout counter at Atkinson's Market is puzzled over my new affection for macaroni and cheese. And, it's certainly not enough that I had to cancel my hair appointment, my nail appointment and my weekly massage! Now, you're expecting me to march down Main Street with a scarlet B on my forehead, announcing that we're officially broke? Our friends, my family—they'll all find out."

Before Mark could reply, a window at the front of the house shattered and a car sped off, tires screeching.

"Stay here!" Mark threw down his screwdriver and fled through the open garage door, craning his neck to catch sight of the culprit.

Leigh Ann ignored him, followed anyway. "What happened?"

He whipped around to her. "I thought I told you to stay in the garage?" Frustrated, he added, "Did you see it? The car?"

Eyes wide, Leigh Ann shook her head. "No, I didn't," she said, joining Mark on the sidewalk, who now stood gazing at the jagged edges of what was left of their front bedroom window, the one where the baby was sleeping.

"Oh my goodness, Hudson!" Leigh Ann whirled and ran back inside.

Despite the sudden noise and being surrounded by glass shards, her nephew slept soundly—totally unaware of the danger he'd been in, or the large rock that lay on the carpeted floor.

Mark scrambled to follow her, stopping at the doorway to catch his breath. "Is he all right?"

"I think so," she answered, lifting Hudson from the bed. She examined him carefully before nestling the tiny boy to her chest. "He seems unscathed."

Mark's eyes filled with despair. "Are you sure?" He moved to the glass-filled crib and yanked the sheet from the bed, wadded it up and marched to the trash bin in the garage where he angrily dumped the evidence.

Leigh Ann followed on his heels. "Maybe you shouldn't do

that until we call the police. They might want pictures," she warned.

"We're not calling the police," he told her.

"Why not? We need to report—"

"I said no."

Leigh Ann felt a sick feeling inside her stomach when she saw his face, the way his eyes clouded as he looked her way. That's when she knew.

Mark still wasn't telling her everything.

11

K aryn stood in front of her bookcase, her hands parked on her hips. She scanned the worn spines, needing to fill another lonely evening.

At least Grayson's return to Alaska had served to reignite her reading habits. In the weeks since he'd been gone, she'd devoured nearly twenty of her old favorites, rereading her Hemingways, some Jodi Picoults, a lot of Debbie Macombers and a few Elin Hildebrands. Her online account activity soared as she filled her e-reader with dozens more. Anything to escape thinking about him, wondering what he was doing, what he had for dinner and if he was happy with his choice to leave her.

And, if she was honest with herself, a much better alternative to her earlier experiments with *escape in a bottle*.

Yeah, that had gone well.

Anesthetizing her pain in secret was an option that would only lead to destruction. She knew that. She'd already promised herself she'd never to go down that path again.

The truth was, life could deal some hard blows. She had a choice—either wallow, or find a way to be happy.

Miss Trudy recommended registering with an online dating

service. "Dear, you just need to get out there again," she'd urged. "When you get bucked off, you simply need to climb back up, take those reins and ride again."

Karyn shook her head, laughed.

Perhaps her love life resembled a wild-west rodeo, but she wasn't looking for a man to lasso her heart. Not now—and maybe not ever again. Her dad had found a way to be happy as a single. Surely she could do the same.

It took effort, but she forced herself to refocus on her books, letting her fingers drift across the spines until she landed on *The Lion, The Witch, and The Wardrobe*. She'd enjoyed the C.S. Lewis classic multiple times. The allegory about four young siblings who step inside a wardrobe closet and retreat into a make-believe world where good triumphs over evil would provide the perfect escape.

Karyn nestled on the sofa with her book, a bowl of buttered popcorn and diet cola. Deep into chapter four, her attention was diverted by a loud banging on her front door.

Alarmed as to who it could be at this hour and why they didn't just ring the doorbell, she tossed her book aside and scrambled for the entryway. "Okay, okay—I'm coming," she hollered.

On the other side of her door stood her neighbor from down the street, a woman who looked eerily like Mrs. Kravitz from the *Bewitched* reruns she and her sisters used to watch on television.

"Honey, did you know you have a broken sprinkler that's flooding the street?" She pointed.

Sure enough, the lane in front of her home rivaled the Wood River during spring run-off.

Her neighbor was quick to point out the obvious. "You're going to have to fix it."

"I—uh, yes. I will. I mean, I'll try." She bit her lip, quickly pondering her limited options given it was after business hours. "Thanks for letting me know. I'll take care of it." She bid the woman on her doorstep goodbye and retrieved her phone from the kitchen counter, quickly dialed her dad. Unfortunately, the call went to voicemail.

Not to be dissuaded, she scrolled her contacts until she found Mark's name and dialed. Her brother-in-law wasn't known for his mechanical ability, but hey—beggars couldn't be choosers.

"Hey, Karyn—what's up?"

"Leigh Ann? What are you doing answering Mark's phone?"

Her sister nearly huffed. "Why wouldn't I? He's my husband."

Karyn studied the shelf where the framed photo of her and Grayson used to be. "Well, doesn't matter. Is he around? I need his help. My sprinklers are broken and one is shooting water several feet in the air which is causing a mini-flood in the street. I need help turning it off until I can get someone out here to fix it tomorrow."

Her sister paused on the other end. "Well, he's sound asleep. I'd wake him but he's not likely to know how to help. We hire all our yardwork done—have for years. Did you go in the garage and turn off the switch in the panel box?"

"No, I didn't," she admitted, mentally chastising herself for not coming up with that solution on her own. "I'll go do that now," she told her sister.

"Good. I'll stay on the line."

Karyn hurried into the garage and opened the cover on the control box, turned the dial to off. "Okay, I turned the sprinklers off. Let me check to see if it worked." She opened the garage door and saw that the mini-geyser in her front yard continued to spew. "Drat! It didn't work. The water is still shooting high into the air, and it's causing a flood in the street. What am I going to do? Do you know anyone else I can call?"

"Look," Leigh Ann said. "Don't panic. We'll figure this out. Hey, hold on a minute—"

The line went dead.

Just when Karyn was about to hang up, Leigh Ann picked back up. "Okay, I know what you need to do."

"Yeah, what's that?" Another of her neighbors was now peeking out her window. Unfortunately, no one came outside and offered to help her.

"I googled it," Leigh Ann told her. "Listen, there's a box buried somewhere in your yard. Lift the lid and inside you'll find a valve. Turn that and it will manually turn the water off. Look, do you need me to come over? I can look—"

"No, that's okay. I got it, thanks."

Karyn ended the call, slipped her phone in her pants pocket and headed outside to look for the box.

She didn't have to look far. The box was located near the light pole next to the road. With determination, Karyn took a deep breath, knelt down and lifted the square green lid.

Inside was nothing but a pool of water, barely visible except for the street light. She cringed. Who knew what could be in that dark water?

There was little choice but to roll up her sleeve and delve in.

Karyn swirled her hand in the cold water until her fingers landed on what felt like some sort of spigot. She grasped the handle and yanked.

Nothing.

Why can't anything be easy?

Angry, she gave the handle another jerk. Hard, this time.

All of a sudden, water gushed, gurgled and then sprayed with such force into her face, the pressure knocked her back.

She was soaked—and totally ticked off.

Karyn struggled to get up, now drenching wet. "Fine!" she yelled out loud.

She marched across the sidewalk, now ankle-deep in water, wishing she'd thought to bring along a flashlight.

That's when her feet slipped out from under her and she went down—hard.

White lightning pain immediately shot through her ankle.

"Ouch!" Hair dripping, she wrestled into a position to get a look. Her ankle had blown up to the size of a small football and was nearly the same color. Tears pooled in her eyes and she bit her bottom lip to keep from sobbing.

She leaned and retrieved her phone from her back pocket, cursed when she saw the shattered face. No amount of pushing the button made the darn thing turn on.

Now what?

She looked around. The sky was really dark now and no one knew she was on the ground and unable to walk on her own. Leigh Ann would no doubt call to check on the fix and see if it worked, but she wouldn't even be able to answer.

Her only choice was to shimmy through the water-filled lawn and try to make it back inside her house.

Whimpering, she turned over and pulled herself with one elbow, then the next—which seemed to work better than using her good knee to assist. The process was slow, and she was in excruciating pain. Her ankle throbbed more with every attempt to move forward.

She was crying now, for real. In fact, a good old-fashioned scream lodged in her throat, demanding release.

Why hold back? There was no one out here at this awful time of night. There was no one for her period. And now there were two geysers shooting water into the air and she was on her own.

Despair flooded the empty space inside her. She planted an elbow—pulled.

A splashing sound caught her attention—the sound of someone running through the water.

Karyn squinted trying to make out who was coming toward her when two arms scooped her up.

"You okay?" The voice was that of a male. "Are you hurt?"

She swiped at her eyes as he carried her into the open garage and laid her down.

"The light switch?" he asked.

She pointed. "Over there."

Suddenly, the garage illuminated and she could identify her rescuer—the same man who had punched out that creepy Robert Nygard, the producer who had visited Sun Valley earlier in the year and stayed at the lodge—the movie mogul who couldn't keep his hands to himself.

"You seem to be in the habit of saving damsels in distress," she remarked, swallowing a sob. *Or at least this one,* she thought, wincing as he examined her ankle.

"I don't think it's broke," he told her. "The way the area around your foot blackened and swelled, I suspect you've torn some ligaments. You definitely need to see a doctor, get an x-ray." He lifted her again and headed back in the direction of the street.

"Could you at least tell me your name before I let you carry me off? By the way, if you have a rap sheet of any sort, I'd prefer for you to simply call my sister." Karyn held up her shattered phone. "I seem to have killed my phone."

"I haven't murdered anyone, if that's what you're asking. Not that I might not have wanted to once or twice."

Karyn couldn't help but smile. She'd felt the same lately. "But you do punch people?"

"Only if someone needs it."

"Do you have a name?" she asked.

He looked to be in his late forties with careless black hair and warm brown eyes. A slow grin played at his mouth as he carefully loaded her in his car—a gray Range Rover with plush leather seats that smelled new.

Karyn audibly groaned as she attempted to straighten her ankle.

"You might want to quit trying to move that," he warned, handing off the seatbelt into her hand.

She felt her cheeks flush at the way he was looking at her. "Look, I don't do men anymore," she started, then seeing the puzzled look on his face, "I mean, I don't do women either." She shook her head. "What I am trying to say is that I—"

"Not trying to jump your bones, ma'am. Just getting you to the doctor."

Karyn lifted her chin, her face in full-flame mode now. "That's not what I meant. I simply want to convey right up front that if you are being so nice because you think—"

"I think you might be one of those who turn opening a can of soup into a ten-minute performance, complete with intermission." Deep dimples sprouted inside the graying beard stubble alongside his mouth as he grinned at her.

She feigned insult. "Oh, really? Well, nothing could be less accurate. I can assure you I'm not prone to drama."

"Is that so?" He closed the door and walked around the front of the car to the driver's side, opened the door and slid in.

He pulled out his phone and made a call about the water, which she appreciated. But what if she'd miscalculated? Maybe it wasn't so smart to get in a car with a stranger, even if he had deep, thoughtful eyes and a slow smile. "Where are you from anyway? I mean, I don't see you around much—here in Sun Valley. I know just about everyone, even the seasonal residents. Are you visiting?"

He didn't answer. Instead, he raked his hand through his thick, slightly curly black hair, started the engine, then reached and turned on the radio. A familiar tune filled the car.

Puzzled, she glared across the seat. "That's it? Instead of answering, you're going to rock out to Van Halen?"

"Yeah. You a fan?" He gunned the engine.

She thought a minute. Was she? She liked some of Sammy Hagar's stuff, possibly more than Eddie Van Halen's influence, but—

"Not a trick question." He tried to smother a smile. "You either do or you don't."

Karyn leaned against the seat, closed her eyes against her building frustration. "Look, right now the only thing I like is feeling no pain. And, I feel a lot of pain—so, maybe we should just focus on getting me to the hospital." She opened her eyes, glanced his way. "And your name. You still haven't told me your name."

Clearly amused, he casually flung his hand over the steering wheel and put the car in gear. "Fair enough. Zane Keppner. Photographer from Dallas. And you?"

"Karyn Macadam—former wife of a dead Olympic star, broken engagement to a backcountry pilot who preferred fatherhood, all-around good girl and best friend to all. Now, can we please just get to St. Moritz?"

12

"I'm sorry, Leigh Ann. There's no way I'm leaving my son in your care when someone is burning your rose bushes and breaking your windows." Joie kissed the top of her baby's downy-soft head as she marched across the church parking lot. "Just no way."

"But—"

"No, buts. I can't risk anything happening to him. You, of anyone, should understand."

Okay sure, her sister was right. In the same situation, she'd have made an identical decision when Colby was little. Still, it smarted to know she'd just been fired through no fault of her own, and lost desperately needed income—a disturbing pattern she had unprecedented lack of control over.

That was the dig. As a kid, she'd believed in fairytales, that fantasy of what life would be, white dress, prince charming who would carry you away to a castle on a hill. She would lie in bed at night and close her eyes with complete and utter faith. Santa Claus, the Tooth Fairy, Prince Charming, they were so close she could taste them. Unfortunately, often a girl grows up and is forced to face the fact that life is not always the lovely story she wants it to be.

Instead, her son was miles away facing danger. Mark was draped over the sofa on a Sunday morning, a glass of scotch in hand, seemingly unable (or unwilling) to look defeat in the eye and stare it down—to rally and save the day. And, somehow she and her husband were now the social pariahs of Sun Valley with some unknown creep pulling dangerous pranks to get even.

Still, it was hard to let go of that fairy tale entirely because there was always a reason to cling to the smallest bit of hope that one day you might open your eyes to find life had turned out the way you designed in your head.

Leigh Ann lifted her chin a bit while following her sister up the sidewalk leading to where Brother John stood at the entrance to Grace Chapel. "Morning, ladies!" He leaned and peeked at little Hudson who was busy gnawing on his dimpled fist. "My, the little guy is growing."

Joie beamed with pride. "And he's nearly sleeping through the night."

Inside, they made their way up the aisle to join Karyn and their dad in a pew near the front of the church.

"Karyn! Oh my goodness—what happened? You told me it was just a little sprain." Leigh Ann pointed to her sister's leg. "You're wearing a cast."

Their dad nodded. "Yes, she broke her ankle while trying to fix her sprinklers.

Joie scowled. "You tried to fix the sprinklers yourself? Why didn't you just call someone?"

Leigh Ann cleared her throat. "She tried. We thought she could turn off the water herself."

"It's nobody's fault. Accidents happen." Karyn shifted to get comfortable.

Leigh Ann scooted into place next to her sister, nested her Coach purse under the pew in front of her. "I can't believe you didn't call me and let me know it was broken. Does it hurt? I mean, I'm sure it hurts—how are you handling the pain?"

"The doctor prescribed some narcotics, but I'm fine without them at this point. Over-the-counter medications seem to be doing the trick for now."

"What are you even doing here?" Leigh Ann asked her. "Shouldn't you be at home with your leg up?"

Their dad grabbed the hymnal from the rack. "I suggested the same."

Leigh Ann opened her mouth to further reprimand her sister, but quickly decided against pushing the issue. It was her unfortunate advice that had landed her sister in this situation in the first place.

GATHERING for Sunday lunch out at the ranch was a long-established family tradition. Today was no different, despite the fact Karyn's entire leg was now aching. In fact, her ankle was throbbing so much she snuck off to the bathroom, popped the lid on the little bottle tucked inside her purse, and downed a painkiller —just a half of one to ease the pulsating pain that made it hard to breathe.

Yes, she'd made a promise to herself not to take any more pills, but that was before she felt like someone was stabbing her ankle with a screwdriver. Besides, this was different. She wasn't slipping into the dangerous territory of self-medicating emotional grief. This was real pain—physical pain—and why the doctor had written out a script and handed it over.

Thankfully, within minutes of taking the medication, her pain subsided, allowing her to join her sisters in the kitchen with a smile, albeit perched on a stool at the counter with her leg up.

Leigh Ann moved to the sink, motioning for Joie to help her clean the tomatoes. "I could use some help in here."

"Hold on to your cookie jar, sugar! I'm coming." Joie finished checking on Hudson, who was sleeping in the pack 'n play in the adjoining living room, before joining them in the kitchen. She'd changed out of her church clothes and now wore her hair in a ponytail with a baseball cap. "So, that was a little obvious you sending Nicole with Dad. You worried he's going to get lost up on the mountain again?" She laughed.

"No, smarty pants. Granted, Daddy's not getting any younger. I constantly worry about him up there, especially when he ignores advice and heads up the mountain alone. But I'd hoped for some alone time for the three of us. It's been ages since we've just talked."

"Talking can be overrated," Joie teased. "What I need these days is sleep."

"Ah—I remember what it was like," Leigh Ann told her. "Just remember this intense motherhood season is short. Soon, you'll be wishing you could get up in the middle of the night and hold them close again." She blinked back emotion before turning to the sink.

Karyn repositioned her leg on the nearby stool. "What do you hear from Colby?"

"Nothing for weeks. Then finally last Tuesday he made contact and we had a chance to Facetime. He looked good, like he's eating well and sleeping. He admitted he's putting in long hours, says he barely has a moment to think about missing us." She released a heavy sigh. "I wish we could say the same."

Joie picked up a tomato and ran it under the running water. "And Mark? How's he doing these days? Does he have any idea who is behind all the threatening behavior?"

"No, but we're not terribly worried," Leigh Ann told them, despite the look on her face that said she clearly was. "Rory Sparks and his team down at the police station seem to be on top of the investigation. They'll find out who's doing all this, and there will be stiff consequences."

Joie turned the water off. "I don't know. Rory isn't exactly Magnum P.I. More like Barney Fife."

"Now you're just being mean," Karyn chastised. "I grew up with Rory."

"Yeah, he was sweet on you in school," Leigh Ann reminded. "If I recall correctly, he decorated your locker with hearts in the eighth grade."

Karyn raised her eyebrows, signaling she didn't find the story amusing. "Oh my goodness, that was years ago. My point is, I know Rory will do everything in his power to do his job. He's a nice guy."

"I didn't claim he wasn't a nice guy," Joie countered. "I just know I've had to interact with him on occasion relating to some of my cases, and well—" She paused, gazed out the window above the sink. "Of course, you may be right. He may well unlock the mystery." Then, under her breath, "Eventually."

Leigh Ann busied herself chopping a tomato. "You know, these beefsteaks are looking pretty good. Perhaps it's time I made a trip to Hagerman and brought back some bushels—"

"No!" Joie and Karyn cried out in unison.

Joie gave her a look. "We're not canning tomatoes again this year, no matter what guilt trip you lay on us."

Karyn nodded. "I agree. I still have jars in my pantry left over from last summer." She laughed. Thanks to the pill, her ankle pain had completely subsided.

Leigh Ann paused her chopping. "Fine," she said. "I suppose the same goes for my other canning efforts? Neither of you wants any of my pickled cucumbers?"

Joie pulled out the lasagna pan from the cupboard under the counter. "Don't go too far. We didn't say that." She looked across the counter. "Did we, Karyn?"

A satisfied look crossed Leigh Ann's face. "Ha—maybe I'll make you wait until Christmas. Gift you some then. But only if you're good." She turned to Joie. "And only if you update us on your relationship with Clint."

She rolled her eyes. "There's nothing to tell. Do I need to keep reminding you we're just friends?"

Leigh Ann grinned. "Friends—with privileges. Babysitting, fixing things around the house, stopping by and bringing you coffee and pastries from Bistro on Fourth. Just friends . . ." She lifted her eyebrows and let her voice trail off with meaning.

Joie waved her off. "Stop. We are—just friends." She paused, then turned to Karyn. "So, I heard some guy drove you to the hospital? What was all that about?" She looked across the kitchen, waiting.

Karyn glanced between her sisters. "Well, it's not the story you two are hoping for. I'd just as soon pop a man's head off than think about him in any sort of romantic way, these days. But I am grateful my new neighbor showed up and took me to the hospital. I was trying to shimmy across the lawn with my elbows, which I don't exactly recommend. In retrospect, I'd never have made it up the steps to my front door."

Leigh Ann arranged the sliced tomatoes on a plate. "Hey, Joie. Check the lasagna, would you?"

Joie grabbed a hot pad from the counter. She bent and opened the oven door. Immediately, an aroma of tomato, basil and garlic permeated the air. "Mmnn . . . looks done to me."

Leigh Ann shoo'ed her out of the way and motioned toward a bottle of wine on the counter. "Uncork that, would you?"

Joie parked her hands on her hips. "Anything else on your to-do list, Sargeant Princess?"

Karyn cleared her throat. "Maybe we should wait for Dad and Nicole?"

Leigh Ann carried the steaming dish to the counter. "Nope. They have their own pan waiting in the oven." She opened a kitchen drawer, dug out three forks and handed off one to each of them. "Dig in."

Grinning ear-to-ear, Joie clasped her chest. "What? No fine china?"

Leigh Ann gave her a look. "Oh, would you please get over yourself!"

All banter aside, never once did one of Leigh Ann's lasagnas actually make it to the table for dinner. No matter what was going on or how mad they might be at each other—it was tradition for all of them to sit at the counter and eat the steaming pasta dish as soon as she pulled the pan from the oven to cool, often burning their tongues on their first bites.

Leigh Ann made the lasagna from a recipe left by their mother, with olives and over-ripened roma tomatoes, spinach, five cheeses, and something else she wouldn't ever confess to no matter how often they tried to ply the secret out of her.

Their dad swore he walked in once and saw her adding chocolate chips to the bottom layer of noodles. The girls had spent years, cumulatively, searching for a sign of the sweet morsels to no avail. Now that they were older, and presumably a bit wiser, they realized he might have been messing with them.

Joie took a large bite as she climbed on the stool next to Karyn. She popped her cheeks out and tried to cool the lasagna already in her mouth, then shoveled more inside. "So, what's his name?" she asked, her mouth still full.

Karyn held her fork midair. "Who?"

Leigh Ann leaned across the counter, picked a piece of olive from the other end of the pan and tossed it inside her mouth. "The neighbor who took you to the hospital. What's his name?"

Karyn dug a big bite out of the middle of the large pan. Leigh Ann looked at her with annoyance. She hated when anyone took lasagna from the middle of the pan.

"Zane Keppner," Karyn answered, ignoring Leanne's stare.

Often, those looks from Leanne prompted Karyn to issue an apology. But one bite and she stopped caring what her older sister thought. The gooey, cheesy mess, sweet and salty with the first taste. The tomatoes as sweet as strawberries, the noodles buttery tender. It reminded her how hungry she was. It reminded her she had failed to eat anything all day. She swallowed and scooped another large bite. "He lives in the place across the street."

Leigh Ann scowled. "I don't know him." She turned to Joie. "Do you know him?"

Joie shook her head. "No. Must be a seasonal tourist. But then you say he's living in your neighborhood?"

Karyn nodded. "He says he's a photojournalist from Dallas. A nurse recognized him and told me he's an author, travel documentarian who focuses on the exploration of international culture and cuisine—is often published in the *New Yorker*, *Travel + Leisure* and *Conde Nast*."

Joie licked her fork. "A celebrity?"

Karyn shook her head. "Oh, I don't think so."

Her younger sister pulled out her iPhone and tapped out something on the tiny screen.

"What are you doing?" Karyn asked her, scowling.

"Looking him up."

Leigh Ann peeked over her youngest sister's shoulder. "What does it say?"

Karyn gave them both a stern look. "Stop. You two are acting like the Dilworth sisters."

Joie studied the small screen, stopped chewing. "Wow! I think your guy is better known than you think."

She set her fork down. "First of all, he's not *my* guy. Second, and to clarify, I don't think anything really. I don't even know the man."

"Well, half of America does." Joie gave her a smug grin. "He's a top-ranked travel essayist, who is winning all kinds of awards for, and I quote, "expanding palates and horizons in equal measure." This says several cable channels have made him offers for television programs, all of which he's turned down."

"You're lucky the media didn't pick up on the story. I can see the headlines now—wife of former Olympic hopeful cooks something up with celebrity travel and culinary author."

Karyn held up her open palms in surrender. "Okay, stop. For real—I'm not kidding."

Joie frowned. "Why are you being so touchy?" She pointed to the pan. "Just eat some more lasagna, cranky pants." She looked over at Leigh Ann. "Goodness, he's cute, though—huh?"

Leigh Ann nodded in agreement. "In a bad-boy sort of way, yeah. Mark never looked like *that* in a leather jacket."

"And those eyes—smoldering and deep." Joie flashed a wide smile over at Karyn. "Girl, you might want to rethink that whole *I'm not interested* thing."

Karyn shoved a huge bite inside her mouth. "Yeah?" she said while chewing. "You first. Unless you think Clint's willing to wait forever."

As if on cue, Hudson woke and started crying.

Joie jumped up and went to him, picked her son up and rocked him. He immediately quieted. "What's the matter, sweet boy, you hungry?" She expertly reached beneath her shirt and undid her bra with one hand. "Just wait until you're old enough to eat lasagna. You have no idea what you're missing."

The back door opened and their dad appeared with Nicole trailing behind. "Hey, what's this?" He sniffed the air and made a beeline for the counter. "Lasagna?"

Karyn leaned back, not bothering to protest as he took the fork from her hand and dug in.

Leigh Ann laughed. "Yours is in the oven, Dad."

Karyn half-listened to their animated chatter, while her mind drifted back to the man who had rescued her—twice.

So, he was some hotdog food author—pun intended. Frankly, she would never have guessed it. Celebrities were all about ratings, branding and image. Dean had sure loved a little public adoration.

Zane seemed to be the exact opposite.

He'd definitely down-played his profession, told her he was simply a photojournalist. Then there was the way he carried her through those sliding emergency room doors, not bothering to stop and read the rules, or get permission. With impressive authority, he marched her past a squawking intake clerk to an empty bed, curtains drawn back, and brashly laid her down, taking care not to hurt her injured ankle.

For a moment or two, she'd been a fair maiden swept from danger by an anachronistic swashbuckling pirate who was not only rakishly handsome, but covered in tattoos and smelled of salty air and the wild sea.

That said, she was pretty sure if someone had the nerve to call him macho to his face, he'd see it as a horrifying accusation.

She remembered back to their first encounter a few months ago. He'd shown up at the film site when the producer was getting out of hand and wouldn't back off, no matter what she said. Without a single word spoken, he landed that jerk on the ground with one much-deserved punch, then simply jogged away.

She'd never known his identify—until the night he carried her into the hospital.

She couldn't tell if the rush of heat she now felt in her gut was the recollection or the painkiller. Either way, she had to admit Zane Keppner was definitely memorable.

13

J oie stood outside the Sun Valley Stables office, stroking Fresca's silky neck. "So boy, you ready for this rodeo?" she asked the gelding she'd spent months training.

The horse knickered softly in response.

"Well, then let's do this." As excited as she was to spend some much needed time in the saddle, she looked over at Clint, feeling conflicted.

"Go," he told her. "We'll be just fine." He gently patted the baby's back, his face still dusty from the day's work. "Won't we little buddy?"

"You sure? Because he was a little fussy earlier and—"

"Go!" Clint waved her off, a grin playing along his strong jawline with that perpetual stubble.

Joie smiled back at him, slipped her foot into the stirrup and pulled herself into the saddle. As if by magic, her shoulders relaxed. Normally, she didn't let circumstances get her down, but she'd been feeling the strain of balancing a full-time law practice and motherhood, especially lately. Finding childcare was proving more difficult than she'd expected.

Until Joie could find a reliable babysitter, Leigh Ann had

agreed to watch Hudson at Joie's house—not ideal, but better than leaving him at her sister's house with all the strange stuff going on. Joie couldn't imagine anyone who would actually want to harm her sister or brother-in-law. Common sense told her the perpetrator was a local who likely wanted to send a message—communicate they were not happy with what Mark had tried to pull off with Preston, USA. That said, the broken glass falling into Hudson's crib was a turning point, forcing a change. Just to be on the safe side.

On those occasions when Leigh Ann's schedule prohibited her from babysitting, Clint and her Dad had both stepped in. The juggling act was not ideal. No doubt she'd have to find a permanent solution, the sooner the better.

Clint cleared his throat. "So, are you going sit in that saddle and stare at us, or are you going to take a ride?"

"Okay, okay—I'm going." Joie gave one last look, waved goodbye before pressing her heels into Fresca's side, urging the horse forward. With the click of her tongue, she drove the prized gelding into a soft lope, past fences and outbuildings into the open space leading up Dollar Mountain.

By the time Fresca's hooves crested the rock cropping west of the footbridge, a familiar tingle trickled down Joie's spine. How had she ever gone so long without riding?

In many ways, she no longer resembled the Joie who used to skydive, race motorcycles and ride through an arena completing the barrels in less than sixteen seconds. That girl was gone. In her place, there was now a woman who relished quiet, late-night hours spent in a rocking chair staring at her sleeping infant son.

If someone had told her a year ago where she'd be today, she'd have never believed it. Yet, while she missed her former life, she wouldn't trade being Hudson's mother for anything.

In the months leading up to his birth, she'd often wondered if she was up for the job, especially given her history. But the lessons had come quick and strong and she no longer doubted her sufficiency. Sure, she still struggled with how often to feed him, what brand of diapers were best, and whether to rush him to the doctor at the first sign of what she thought might be a sniffle —just like all new moms.

Deep down, she'd learned being a mother had very little to do with simply birthing a child from your body. Motherhood was the melding of two hearts. Her own was now so inexplicably entwined with her infant son's, there was no way to tell where his heartbeats stopped and hers began. No matter what the future held, she vowed to wrap him in a blanket of lifetime comfort, to protect her son and give him everything possible.

Joie reined in Fresca, slowing his gait. She gazed up at the brilliant blue sky, knowing that true commitment took effort and sacrifice—a willingness to risk it all. Nothing, and no one, could ever pull her away from her commitment to Hudson.

With that thought solid in her mind, she made her way to the ridge running along the western crest of Dollar Mountain. From this vantage point, the ribbons of steel-grey stream water in Trail Creek drew a sharp contrast against the purple-hued lupine patches leading to the water's edge.

This valley had a rich heritage, one steeped in gold exploration and mining.

Joie could hardly wait for her son to grow old enough to ride with her. She'd bring him to this very spot and pass on the stories of her ancestors, Asa and Foley Abbott, of their son, Edward Lee Abbott, of his daughter Leona, who had courageously pioneered the Sun Valley area. She wanted Hudson to know how deeply he was rooted in these mountains.

A twig cracked in the distance, pulling her attention to a stand of aspens, their silver-dollar leaves gently blowing in the mountain breeze. At the base of the trees, tall grasses rustled and a raccoon appeared with four kits trailing behind. The raccoon stopped, popped up onto its hind legs and stared at her, fiercely protective and sizing her up.

"Don't worry," she told the raccoon out loud. "We're in this motherhood thing together."

As if the animal understood there to be no danger, the furry black and white creature turned and chittered to her babies before leading her little family down the hillside.

When the raccoons were finally out of sight, Joie gathered the reins and continued down the trail, enjoying a welcome feeling of content.

Hours later, she arrived back at the stables a new woman, vowing to make riding a more frequent diversion from her day-to-day responsibilities.

"Hey, you're back." Clint cradled a sleeping Hudson against his shoulder.

Suddenly, Joie's heart was all up in her throat and she wasn't sure why. She wanted to pretend seeing her friend standing there with her son held close to his chest, rock solid, did nothing to her insides—but she couldn't deny the way her gut tightened at the sight.

With his free hand, Clint reached for the halter and led the horse forward, to the barn door.

Joie dismounted and lifted her son from her friend's arms, kissed the top of the baby's downy head. "Was he any trouble?"

Clint shook his head, a smile tugging at his lips. "Nah, he slept the entire time you were gone, waking just long enough for a bottle."

"Thank you so much for watching him, Clint. That ride was like a drink of water in the desert."

His eyes trained on hers. "My pleasure."

A slightly nervous bubble of laughter caught in her throat as she told him about the raccoons and the lupines, how the views were truly beautiful. "The air just smells better up on the mountain, you know?"

She loved that this man understood what she meant, that they adored horses and shared a reverence for the outdoors. Most especially, she admired the way he cared for her son, and her. Maybe Leigh Ann was right. He would make the perfect—

She reined in her rogue thought. He'd make the perfect *best friend*, she mentally told herself.

As a diversion, she pointed to the filled parking area. "Looks like you've been busy," she commented, as Clint handed Fresca off to one of the groomers.

"Hey, Joie—long time, no see." Patty hooked a lead rope onto Fresca's halter. "Did you have a good ride?"

Joie patted Fresca's hind quarter with her free hand. "I did."

A white sedan lumbered into the yard, parked and out climbed a guy who looked to be about fifty. He wore khaki slacks and a golf t-shirt.

"Hmnn . . . looks like another tourist." Clint grinned. "That's a good thing, I guess. Keeps the doors open."

She smiled back at him. They both knew the stables were a favorite of the resort owner's wife, Nola Gearhart. The doors would remain open regardless of profit margin.

The man in the khakis made his way over, carrying a leather satchel. "Hey," he said, greeting them.

Clint nodded. "Welcome to the Sun Valley Stables. You have a ride booked?"

The man shook his head. "No. I'm looking for Joie Abbott. I was told she'd be here this morning."

A puzzled frown crossed Joie's face. "That's me."

The man looked her over as he opened his satchel. He pulled a set of stapled papers out and handed them to her. "Ms. Abbott —you've been served."

14

Karyn pulled a plate from her cupboard and placed it on the counter, knowing full well delivering cookies to her neighbor wasn't going to be easy, given she'd have to hobble over there in a walking cast. Still, it would be rude not to offer some token of appreciation.

She piled the plate with homemade oatmeal and raisin cookies, worried a foodie like Zane Keppner might not appreciate such a simple recipe. She shook her head, pushed the plate back. Perhaps a better idea was to simply call him.

Wait—she didn't have his phone number.

Karyn stared at the plate, frustrated. Why did she care what a fancy food critic thought? It was the gesture that counted. Especially given the ankle pain she knew would come from the precarious trip across the street.

This was a bad sprain, she quickly justified, when grabbing the half-empty bottle from the counter. She tapped some tablets into the palm of her hand, swallowed one—then a second. Her ankle was an absolute bear if she didn't stay ahead of the pain.

She took a deep breath, pulled the plate into her hands and headed for the door.

As she maneuvered up to his front entry, it dawned on her he might not even be home. In that case, she supposed she could leave them on his doorstep. She reached for the doorbell, but before she could push the button, the door suddenly opened.

"Karyn?"

She looked up into her neighbor's face. "Oh—uh, hello. I wanted to thank you for the other night, so I brought—" She stepped closer, thrust the plate out, nearly dropping it to the ground in the process. "I'm sorry, I—"

Darn this cast! And the pills—the pills didn't help.

She heard him take a deep breath. He reached for the cookies. "Here, I got it."

Leigh Ann and Joie had a point. The guy did have amazing eyes. They were the warm-golden-brown color of pricey cognac and there was a depth, an independence and a way of observing that left her feeling emotionally naked.

Karyn stilled the unfounded panic emerging in her heart and handed over the treats. "I wanted to thank you," she repeated, a bit too quickly.

He slowly nodded, looked her over. "You—uh, you want to come in?"

She promptly shook her head. "No. I mean, well—I'm sure you're busy. And I need to get back." She warned herself to calm down, quit talking herself into a corner.

"Why are you so nervous?"

His comment took her aback. "Nervous? I—I'm not nervous." She silently prayed her eyes would not reveal the lie she'd just told.

"I was just heading out for a photoshoot at the Galena Lodge. You want to join?"

She resisted telling him that she was no longer interested in spending time with men—especially men with those eyes, men she barely knew. Even if he'd been so kind to her, had selflessly taken her to the hospital, staying until he knew she was all right and her family had arrived. Horrified, she heard herself saying, "Well, I haven't eaten yet today."

"Great!" He stepped back and motioned her inside.

As she hobbled her way past him, he lifted the cellophane covering the plate and slid a cookie inside his mouth. "Mmnn —good."

"I hope those don't ruin your appetite. For lunch," she clarified.

"Not likely," he said. "My appetite is pretty healthy." A slow grin pushed through deep dimples. "For lunch."

Karyn nervously broke her gaze and drew her attention to his house. His living room was definitely a masculine space— featuring large elements free of clutter. A coffee-colored leather sectional, tables made of rich, dark wood and immense windows overlooking a deck lined with aspens and small spruce trees. Gunmetal gray walls were lined with crowded bookcases with an overstuffed reading chair wedged in the corner. "Nice place," she commented, noting he apparently was a reader, like her.

"I lease it—temporarily. Came with the furnishings." He followed her line of vision. "Except the books. Those are mine."

"Oh?" The fact he'd leased would answer why she'd never seen a for sale sign go up, or any moving trucks—why she'd never known a new neighbor had moved in. "Well, it's really nice."

Zane rolled up his shirt sleeves. "Look, I'd offer you something to drink, but I'm running a bit late. I understand Galena Summit is about thirty-five minutes north of here. We'd better get going."

"Yeah, sure. Okay." It dawned on her she didn't have her purse. "First, I need to grab my bag. Meet you in the front yard?"

Minutes later, she finished locking her front door, then turned as his garage door opened.

Burr . . .oom. Boom. Boom. Boom.

The rumble of the engine roared louder as Zane pumped the handle and carefully backed a motorcycle down his driveway.

Karyn clutched her hand to her chest. A motorcycle?

Zane grinned as he pulled up alongside her. "Ready?" he yelled over the noise.

"I—I don't ride motorcycles."

Ignoring her protests, he handed her a helmet and motioned for her to climb aboard. "Ah, c'mon. Live a little," he told her, positioning his own helmet in place. He lifted the face guard. "We'll be able to talk to each other through the built-in headsets." He pointed.

Karyn hesitated, unsure what to do. She'd never maneuvered herself onto the back seat of a hog—*is that what you called one of these things?* Especially while wearing a walking cast.

But he was staring at her, daring her to change her mind.

She blinked several times and simply went for it. After securing her purse strap across her chest, she pulled on the helmet and tightened the chinstrap. With her heart pounding, she placed her good foot on the foot peg, then mounted the bike, swinging her cast over the low-slung seat and slipping into place behind Zane taking care not to make contact with the shiny exhaust pipe. Immediately, she smelled gasoline fumes, felt waves of heat coming from the engine.

She wrapped her arms around Zane's waist, then pressed her face against his back and the worn leather of his jacket. Her heart lurched with hesitation, the kind you feel when you climb on the biggest thrill ride at the carnival and suddenly wish you hadn't. She'd likely never have attempted something so fool-hardy without the fake euphoria created by the pills she'd taken.

"Hang on," he shouted into her earpiece.

He gunned the engine and they jetted forward, immediately leaning into a turn in the road. A rush of wind caught her hair sending her tresses flying from beneath her helmet. For a moment, she felt airborne, the way a bird must feel when it soars the sky.

Unable to help herself, she smiled at the feeling of complete freedom.

In minutes, they were out of the neighborhood and onto Sun Valley Road heading into nearby Ketchum, past Bistro on Fourth and Louie's Pizza. At the corner of Main, they stopped at the red light.

Zane's voice came through the headset, "Doing okay?"

"Yes," she hollered back. ""I'm fine."

The drive through the high mountain passes along State Highway 75 climbed steadily to an elevation of over eight thousand feet and provided some of the most stunning scenery known to man—vistas filled with grassy meadows and pines, sagebrush and burbling creeks. If you watched closely, you might even spot a deer or an elk bedded down in the shade outcroppings of aspens, escaping the summer heat.

Galena Summit marked the divide between the Big Wood River and the Salmon River drainage areas with a scenic viewpoint that offered spectacular views of the Sawtooth mountain range and the headwaters of the Salmon River.

The small timbered lodge was a gem-in-the-rough—built in the late forties and a favorite of not only cross country skiing and snowshoeing enthusiasts, but bicycle racers and nature lovers as well.

Zane slowed as they approached the gravel parking lot. He eased into a vacant spot between an SUV and a pickup, pulled off his helmet.

She removed her own helmet, shook out her hair. "That was amazing!" she told him, and she meant it. She hadn't felt like this good since—well, since Grayson had left.

Inside, they met up with the owners, a husband and wife duo known simply as Erin and Don to the locals. As hard as she tried, she couldn't seem to remember their last name, not that it mattered. The important thing was how everyone raved about their food.

Zane moved to the packs on the bike and retrieved a camera bag, which he slung over his shoulder before leading her to a small table out on the deck.

"Do the restaurant owners know? I mean, that you're here and that you are doing an article?" she asked, taking her seat.

Zane shook his head. "Normally, I make my visits incognito. This time, I gave them a heads up. Partly, because Don and I have a little history." He moved into the seat opposite her. "We both grew up in New Jersey."

A man with sandy-colored hair wearing a white chef apron approached. "Hey, guy!"

Zane stood and gave him a hug. "Good to see you again."

"You too, man. It's been too long since I filled up that belly of yours."

Zane laughed. "The only thing that's going to fill me up today is one of those elk burgers I've been hearing about."

"You got it." His friend winked. "And I've got a few surprises."

Zane looked at him appreciatively, then at her. "Don, this is my neighbor, Karyn Macadam."

The chef nodded. "Yeah, we've never formally met, but I know Karyn." He reached to shake her hand. "You work at the Sun Valley Lodge, right?"

"Yeah, been there a little over a year now. Before that—well, before that I lived a different life." She let her voice fade slightly.

Don wiped his hands on a towel tucked into his apron strings. "Well, you two enjoy. I've got to get back to the kitchen. Some big wig is writing an article on the place, and I've got to impress him."

Zane laughed. When they were alone, he looked across the table. "Nice guy."

"Seems so," she said, squeezing a wedge of lemon into a glass of water that had been brought to the table by a waitress. "So, you grew up in New Jersey?"

He ran fingers through thick black curls, some still matted from the helmet. "Yeah."

According to Zane, he was raised in a stable home, where his parents taught him to love music and film. He grew up in the *Mad Men* era, watched his family, neighbors and parents' friends struggle with rapidly changing social mores, the Vietnam war. His dad worked two jobs as a salesman in Brigson's camera store in New York and as a floor manager at a record store. Later, he scored a nice gig at Columbia Records.

"We were a pretty typical suburban family in most ways," he explained. "I was a reader. Our house was filled with good books. Both my parents loved great movies."

A waiter arrived with a tray of food. She placed an elk burger with an enormous mound of French fries in front of Zane. Her lunch was a serving of their much-raved-about pork mojo, a latin-inspired dish made from bone-in pork shoulder marinated with orange and lime juice, oregano, garlic and cumin.

Zane exchanged lens on his camera and popped off a few shots of the food from various angles before returning to his seat. "Looks good, let's eat."

She learned he was a rebellious and bitter teen who desperately wanted to join the counter culture made popular by Kurt Cobain in Seattle, wanted to get high and make artistic music like many of his friends. Unfortunately, he was stuck at home, working at summer jobs and helping his family keep their heads above financial water.

"Most of my friends had rich absentee parents or came from broken homes," he told her. "So, they were free to do whatever they wanted. I deeply resented the relative stability at my house. Unfortunately, I experimented with drugs as soon as I encountered them. I tried to be an underground comedian in one of those dark smoke-filled basement lounges but I was too lazy, undisciplined and stoned to apply myself. Back then, I was a miserable, self-destructive lout."

Wide-eyed, Karyn took a bite of her pork. "You were a druggy?"

He laughed. "Clearly, you were not." He took a bite of his elk burger and paused to chew. "Thankfully, I had parents who wouldn't put up with my crap. They did the whole *tough-love* thing and shoved my butt in a ninety-day rehab program. Scared the poop out of me, frankly. In the end, my father became one of my best friends."

For a moment, he stared out in the distance. "There wasn't a pretentious bone in that man's body. He was never afraid to appear ridiculous or silly for my entertainment. He was incapable of restraining himself from sharing his passions, whether I was old enough to see Dr. Stangelove, for instance, or not. He was never a snob about anything. He was sentimental, but spoke to me as an adult, even when I was just a kid. He enjoyed simple things, and made me understand the joy of good food unfettered with unnecessary embellishments, for example."

Zane shoved a fry inside his mouth. "He applauded cleverness, wit. I aspire to be much the same, though with perhaps a more focused work ethic."

"Do your parents still live in Jersey?"

He swallowed, took a long drink of his beer. "Nah. I was shucking oysters at a raw bar in Seattle when I got word they'd been in a fatal accident. Dad was 47, the age I am now."

She instinctively reached across the table, covered his hand in her own. "I'm so sorry."

He grinned at her, withdrew his hand and patted hers. "Don't be. None of us get out of this journey alive. His time just came a bit early, that's all."

With a puzzled frown, she asked, "That's it? That's your life philosophy? We live, we die, and if we're lucky we don't go too soon?" The anger in her voice surprised even herself. Embarrassed, she quickly busied herself by moving around the corn relish that came with her pork.

"Sorry. Did I touch on a sensitive subject?"

Karyn stared at her plate. "My husband was Dean Macadam."

"Yeah? I'm sorry, I don't believe I know—"

Her head popped up. She gave him an incredulous look. "*The Dean Macadam.*" Still no understanding. "The Olympic hopeful who died up on Baldy?"

"Oh." He shrugged. Not in an uncaring manner, but a gesture that suggested the information didn't warrant an unnecessary change in his demeanor. "I'm sorry that happened to you," he offered, his voice sincere.

She waved off his too-little, too-late expression of sympathy. "It's just—well, I think it's a big deal. When you lose someone you love, I mean."

He sat silent for several seconds, before leaning forward. "Yes, but it's far more tragic to quit living after they leave."

The comment burned. "Look, you might be considerably older than me, and that makes you believe you're a lot wiser, but you don't know me."

"Yeah, maybe not." He shrugged, with a gleam in his eyes. "Then again, it's entirely possible I know you better than you know yourself."

15

"What do you mean he's suing you for custody?" Leigh Ann slammed the kitchen drawer shut with her hip. "Has Andrew Merrill lost his ever-loving mind?"

"Can he even do that?" Karyn asked. "I thought he relinquished custody."

Joie leaned against Leigh Ann's kitchen counter, rubbed at her temples. "He's Andrew Merrill. He can do anything."

Leigh Ann snatched the papers from the counter. Peering through her new reading glasses, she read the contents. "Says here he and his wife have reconciled?"

"Yeah," Joie said, miserably. "Can you believe that horn dog convinced his wife to return? After me—and all the others?"

Karyn grimaced. "There were others? That's just, well—awful." She made a gagging noise while poking a finger down her throat.

"What does Maddy say about all this?" Leigh Ann demanded.

"She's filing a response," Joie carefully explained. "We intend to fight this, of course. I'd rather die than let that creep get his hands on my Hudson."

Karyn tucked a stray hair behind her ear. "Surely, he won't win."

"No, he won't prevail," Joie assured her. "We're moving for an emergency hearing and a motion to dismiss his action. We're filing the waiver he signed as an exhibit where he clearly stated he was not interested in being part of any of Hudson's life. And I'll file an affidavit that he pressed for me to get an abortion. That at no time did he display any intent to co-parent this child."

Karyn got up, hobbled over to her younger sister. She put her arms around her shoulders. "I know this is a hassle. But please don't worry. Justice will prevail and we'll be right by your side the entire time." She winced at the throbbing in her ankle.

Leigh Ann immediately picked up on her pain, studied her curiously. "You still hurting? When do you go back to your doctor?"

Karyn turned her attention to getting herself a glass of water. "Later this week. He said he'd remove the cast then, if everything looked okay."

Leigh Ann nodded, tossed the papers back on the counter. "Well, Joie—all I can say is I knew that Andrew Merrill was trouble the minute I met him. In fact—"

Joie groaned. "Oh c'mon, don't start."

Ignoring her protests, Leigh Ann continued. "He's nothing like Clint," she argued. "Now that guy is husband material. And he'd make a great father." She gave Joie a pointed look. "Have you seen the statistics? You don't want Hudson to grow up without a dad. I'm telling you that, right now."

Joie visibly pulled on her hair in frustration. "Look, I need to go." She grabbed the papers, shoved them inside her bag. "I've got to pick up Hudson."

"Is Dad watching him?"

Joie didn't try to hide her impatience. "No. He's with Clint."

Leigh Ann's eyes sparkled with smug indignation. "I rest my case." She turned to Karyn. "Am I right? He'd make a great dad."

She wiped the counter. "You both know I'm right," she called out as Joie headed for the door, slamming it behind her.

Alone, Leigh Ann turned her attention to Karyn. "She's so touchy."

"She's upset," Karyn said, defending her sister. "You would be too if you had someone trying to take your kid away."

"Oh, that Merrill character might be some hotshot attorney, but he'll never win. No judge in his or her right mind would grant parental rights to someone like that." She paused. "I mean, I'm right. He won't win, will he?"

Karyn let out a heavy sigh. "I hope not."

Leigh Ann folded the wash cloth and set it by the side of the sink. "Hey, Karyn. I have something I need to ask you." This was the last thing she wanted to do, but she had no choice. "I need a favor."

Karyn looked at her warily. "Yeah, what's that?"

Leigh Ann fought to look nonchalant. "As you know, Mark and I are in—well, we're swimming upstream these days. We have plenty of financial resources to fall back on. Mark was a careful investor." She hated lying to her sister, but what choice did she have? "It's just that—well, having him here in the house every day is driving me crazy. He's struggling with a little depression." Leigh Ann hated throwing Mark under the bus, but wasn't this all his fault in the first place? She went on. "Anyway, now that I am no longer at the tourism council, I need something to fill my days, get me out of here. You know?"

Karyn frowned. "Okay," she said slowly, clearly wondering what all that had to do with her.

"Especially now. With all this free time on my hands, I seem to spend every waking moment worrying about Colby. You know?" Okay, that was another cheap shot, but she was desperate.

Leigh Ann decided to jump in the ice pond, face the freezing water, so to speak. "I need you to give me a job."

Karyn gave her an incredulous look. "At the lodge?"

"Yes, I saw a temporary job posted online for someone to cover for the registration desk clerk while she's out on leave. I'd be perfect. And I'm available immediately."

"Oh, Leigh Ann—I don't know if that's such a good idea. I mean, you just don't hire someone you can't fire."

"What does that mean?" she asked, laughing. "You think you'd have to fire me?"

Karyn quickly shook her head. "No—no, it's not that. I only mean I don't think it's a good idea for you to work for me."

"We'd be working *together*," Leigh Ann corrected. "And you know I'd do a good job. Besides, I need this employment or I wouldn't be asking. A lot of people are mad at us and it's going to be difficult for me to land anything right now. You know that. Besides, it's actually far less risky to hire someone you trust will do a good job. Do you honestly believe hiring someone off the street to be the first face your guests encounter is a better idea?" She gave her sister a convincing smile, knowing she had her there.

Karyn remained wary. "I—I'll have to think about it."

Leigh Ann took her sister's empty water glass to the sink. "Great! I can start on Monday."

MARK FINISHED SHAVING and got dressed, hearing Leigh Ann's voice in his head. "Mark, go with the blue tie. Blue is a power color."

That woman he'd married could drive him up the wall with all her opinions and advice. Yes, she was often right. But he also knew her incessant need to have everything in life in its proper place was nothing more than insecurity. He'd learned that yet again last summer, when she thought he was having an affair with Andrea DuPont, his business partner.

He hated the place they were in right now, and it was all his fault. He'd seriously miscalculated a business opportunity and now he was the pariah of Sun Valley. No one would take his calls. No one would wave on the street, or even talk to him, for that matter. It was hard not to lose hope, to not believe he was finished in this town.

Which is why when he got the call from Reeve Rusk inviting him to meet him for lunch, he'd jumped at the idea. Mark had long been an admirer of the business mogul, a man who had built a multi-billion-dollar enterprise from the ground up. The idea of meeting with such a man in person had him fussing like Lewinsky in front of Clinton. And you'd better believe, he was ready to go nearly as far to get in bed with this guy.

He grabbed the blue tie and secured it perfectly in place.

This meeting could be the chance of a lifetime—and the single thing that could turn everything around.

Mark pulled into a parking spot on the street in front of the Pioneer Saloon, rethinking his decision not to tell Leigh Ann about this meeting. Secrets were never a good idea, but he didn't want to get his wife's hopes up unnecessarily. If things progressed today, he'd take her someplace special and break the news. They hadn't been out in weeks.

He was a bit surprised at the choice of restaurants suggested by this Rusk guy. No doubt the food was delicious, but unlike the many al fresco dining options people often frequented in the summer, the Pioneer was dark with tables nestled in out-of-the-way spots, some as far back as the kitchen.

Mark took a deep breath, placed his hand on the metal pull and yanked the heavy door open. It took several seconds for his eyes to adjust to the lack of light.

"Mark, there you are!"

Mark turned to the man who had extended his arm. He swallowed his sudden nerves and pasted a smile. "Mr. Rusk. So nice to finally meet in person."

"Call me Reeve." He placed his hand on Mark's back. "I hope you don't mind. I've already got us a table."

Mark followed him to the rear of the restaurant, to a large wooden table located near the stairs leading to the basement level and directly underneath a massive taxidermied moose head.

"Mark, I hope you don't mind. I've invited others to join us." He pointed to the men already at the table. "This is Peter Schmeizer and Tom Murdock."

Mark's fingers went to his collar. He pulled at the fabric that seemed to squeeze his ability to breath. He didn't like surprises.

Reeve motioned for Mark to sit. He took his own seat. "I can see from the look on your face this isn't exactly as you expected. I'd like to cut right to the chase, lay the cards on the table here."

Now Mark was really getting uncomfortable. He'd wanted a business deal proposal, or a job offer at the least. He needed something desperately and wasn't fond of the idea of getting jerked around—even if it was Reeve Rusk doing the yanking.

Reeve held up his open palm. "Let me explain." He planted his elbows on the table, leaned over. "I need something from you. And, I hope you'll agree to help me."

He was curious now. "Okay. I'm open to listening." It was important he not reveal just how anxious he was to do a deal. Not if he was going to have any negotiation power. No doubt Rusk had done his homework and understood his predicament, at least to some extent.

Reeve nodded. "Good." He turned to the gentlemen at the table. "Tom is the general counsel for my holding company. Peter Schmeizer here heads up the white collar crime unit of the FBI in our district."

Mark fumbled his utensils, made a clanging sound. "Sorry, I —uh, a federal agent?"

Mr. Schmeizer looked across the table and smiled. "Actually, I'm Assistant Director of the Corporate Fraud Unit."

Sweat sprouted on Mark's scalp. "Okay." He knew the single

word response sounded lame, but he was totally taken off guard here. He considered taking this meeting might have been his worst mistake to date, and that was saying a lot.

Reeve waved off an approaching waiter. "Give us a few minutes, please?"

The waiter nodded. "Certainly, sir."

Reeve turned his attention back to Mark. "Like I said, I need your help. Have you ever heard the term *pump-n-dump?*

What was this, a test? He shook his head. "I may have." Best to stay noncommittal.

Reeve smiled patiently. "Well, a pump-n-dump is a market manipulation scheme where business owners drive up the price of stocks and then cash out causing the stock to plummet in value."

Peter nodded, pulled at his crisp white shirt cuffs. "Often the scheme involves employing ambitious brokers to cold call unsuspecting investors, selling them worthless stocks. It's a money laundering scheme, of sorts."

Reeve went on. "The end result is overstated income by intentionally understating liabilities and concealing debt through the creation of off balance sheet entities to hide these profits."

"And subsequent tax evasion," Peter added.

Mark frowned. "What does this have to do with me?" He'd cut plenty of corners in his business dealings, but certainly nothing that even closely resembled fraud, especially the magnitude these guys were talking about.

Tom finally broke his silence. "How did you meet Andrea DuPont?"

Mark's gut cinched. "Andrea? Well, let's see. We were introduced at a business expo in San Francisco. We exchanged business cards. Months later, she called and asked if I was interested in an opportunity that could stand to be lucrative. She told me she had a company in her targets, one she wanted to partner with. At least, that's what she said initially. Very soon after, I learned the plan had morphed into a possible take-over."

Mark hated admitting his role in the debacle. His involvement in the Prescott, USA mess did nothing to build the esteem of the gentlemen around this table, he was sure.

"What do you know of her personally?" Tom asked.

Mark glanced between the men, wondering what kind of mud he was slogging into. "Well, very little really. I believe she told me she grew up outside D.C. Said she was the oldest of three children in a tightly-knit Jewish family. According to her curriculum vitae, she graduated summa cum laude at Harvard and went on to work for one of the most well-known management consultant agencies around—Roseburg and Associates. Sometime after, she started Equity Capital Group." That was the bare bones, but all they really needed to know until he better understood what they were after. Andrea was his business associate. While things had not turned out like they'd hoped, he still admired her business acumen.

Peter seemed to pick up on his reluctance. "That's our understanding as well," he said. "Unfortunately," he paused, looked at the others. "Well, Ms. DuPont is not exactly as she purports herself to be."

Mark scowled. "What do you mean?"

"He means," Reeve interrupted. "Andrea DuPont has taken my company for a load of money, whittled at my equity using illegal schemes. As a result, I intend to restore my holdings to their earlier standing, and I've got to take this woman down to do it."

Tom nodded. "And that's where the Feds come in."

"And you," Peter added, looking unnecessarily smug. "We need your help. More importantly, no one must know."

Mark sat back in his chair, nearly speechless. Andrea DuPont? Dirty? That was hard to imagine. He'd worked with her for months. Wouldn't he have known?

When he'd recovered enough to respond, he leaned forward, determined to cover his own butt. "This sounds like some television movie, or something. I mean, if what you say is true and I do what you ask, I sense there could be some danger involved." He nervously cleared his throat. "We've already had some—well, some incidents."

Peter drilled him with a sober look. "Yes, we're aware of the *incidents*. No need to worry. We've already investigated and have identified the culprit. The perpetrator is fairly harmless. An agent is showing up at his house while we speak. He'll be served a warrant, let out on his own recognizance and warned to keep his nose clean in the future."

Mark's eyes widened. "Who?

Reeve steepled his fingers. "Buck Randles."

"The retired school janitor?"

Tom reached for his water glass. "Yes. Apparently, he'd taken a loan on his school retirement funds and had invested. He lost quite a bit in the Preston buy-back."

Mark's heart sunk. It was much easier to think of the investors in the collective, and not have a name, a story, to contend with.

"This is your chance to make all this up to your fellow residents here in Sun Valley—to turn your reputation around," Reeve offered, prodding him to join forces.

As an added incentive, Peter added, "And your opportunity to rinse yourself of any criminal repercussions. We'd provide you with full immunity."

Mark's heart went in his throat. "Me? I didn't do anything."

Reeve nodded. "Let's hope not. Regardless, we need to know your answer. Are you in?"

Mark now knew what that proverbial deer felt like staring into the headlights. His mind raced, his palms turned sweaty. What option did he have, really, but to agree to their proposal?

The message in their looks was absolutely clear. He was either with them, or against them. If he failed to cooperate, they would make his life a living hell. If they brought any sort of charges, even given the fact he was not complicit, he had no money for a legal defense. He'd have to ask Leigh Ann's father for help, and that would not go over big with his wife. Might even deal a fatal blow to their marriage.

The men across the table watched him—waited.

Mark swallowed. "I—yes, I'm in."

16

Joie sat in her desk chair facing the window, staring blankly out at Baldy Mountain and recalling how, during ski season, the mountain was gloriously white, with crisp alpine runs filled with dare-devil skiers. Summer was just as beautiful, but in a much different way. The mountain gave way to shades of green, ribboned with empty ski runs traversed by only a few adventurous mountain bikers seeking a thrill.

The contrast was remarkable, yet predictable. Season by season, the landscape changed—even when the foundation remained the same. Yet in both winter and summer, people on the mountain had to maneuver the terrain to keep from wiping out.

Life was like that. One chapter morphed into another. You had to adapt, or risk crashing. Her dad often claimed you couldn't change the direction of the wind, but you could adjust your sails and still reach your destination.

Still, she could barely swallow these recent changes and the potential fall she feared was coming.

Earlier that morning, she'd met with Maddy to discuss strategy and develop a more concrete plan to respond to

Andrew's insane claim that he should have parental rights restored.

"Darlin', I know you aren't going to like hearing this, but the outcomes in these matters are hard to predict. Too many factors play into a judge's decision, especially when considering blocking a parent from their child."

She knew Maddy was right, but she'd argued anyway. "He's not a parent, he's the sperm donor. Not to be crass, but you and I both know there's more to fathering a child than leaving a few microscopic cells inside a woman and then walking away."

Maddy looked at her with patience. "Yes, sweet thing, but he's going to do everything he can to convince the judiciary he has had a change of heart and now wants to do more. Historically, the courts are reluctant to sever parental rights, even in the case when a parent initially relinquishes. In these cases, they often rule in favor of the petitioning parent, and most particularly when the child is under the age of a year."

That's when she'd lost it, even threw her pen across the conference room table. "How could anyone believe Andrew Merrill is a fit parent? No matter what it takes, I'll make sure he's never a part of *my* son's life!"

"Listen, sweet thing—I've explained the position historically taken by the courts. That said, Mad Dog has snarled with a few junk yard dogs in her day. I fully aim to bite back." She reached across the table, took Joie's hand in her own. "You're going to have to trust me."

Trust.

Joie turned back to her desk, buried her face in her hands. No matter the earnest look on her law partner's face in that meeting, trusting was easier said, than done.

Deep down, she knew Maddy was one hundred percent correct. Yes, Mad Dog Maddy Crane was the best in the business, and she trusted her to do all she could. Yet, her evaluation was spot on—Joie had a legal mountain to climb that was every bit as high as Baldy. The stakes were extremely high. One bad maneuver and Joie would crash and burn.

What she needed was a foolproof plan, one that left nothing to chance. She knew what she had to do.

Jon Sebring looked across the desk. "Are you sure about this? Sometimes difficulties can arise when family members work together, especially if one is supervising the other."

Karyn took a deep breath, looked her boss in the eyes. "Yes, I admit I had some slight reservations, but I'm in a bit of a pinch. My sister really needs this job and it just so happens that Melissa Jaccard is going on maternity leave soon. Leigh Ann could fill in for her at the front desk and be fully trained prior to the Vanguard conference. A win-win. Besides, it's temporary," she told him.

Jon nodded. "It's completely your decision. I hired you as our hospitality director because I trust your judgment."

She appreciated his nod of confidence. "Thank you, Jon."

Leigh Ann was elated when Karyn told her. "That's wonderful news." She drew her into a tight hug. "This will give us the opportunity to spend even more time together."

Karyn didn't feel as upbeat about the whole thing. She couldn't ignore the gnawing feeling she'd been pushed into a decision she'd known better than to make. Leigh Ann had a way of manipulating people into doing exactly what she wanted them to, and no doubt she'd been craftily maneuvered.

Why did she continue to let people trample all over her, especially those she loved most? Her need to please, to avoid conflict, seemed to leave her unable to stand up for herself.

Just the other day, Dean's mom had called to let her know they were wrapping up their tour of Greece and would be home soon. She asked—no subtly demanded—that Karyn rearrange her busy schedule to pick them up at the airport. Never mind they could rent a car, or book a town car. "But we can't wait to see you," Aggie skillfully argued, and she'd relented.

Her sisters certainly knew all her buttons, and they never hesitated to push them to their advantage. "Could you pick up Hudson's eyedrops at the pharmacy for me? It's on your way home." Karyn mentally demonstrated the button notion with an imaginary finger poke in the air.

"I know you're busy, but it would mean so much to Colby if you would send him a box of Idaho Spud candy bars. I'm sure he's homesick and he needs to know his family is thinking about him." Another air poke.

Even her dad, who no doubt loved her dearly, seemed to be unaware how small she felt when they all got together, how hard it was for her to be heard amongst all the noise.

And it wasn't only her family.

"I need a donation." *Poke.*

"I need you to attend this charity dinner." *Poke, poke.*

And the best yet: "I need you to step aside, let me return to Alaska and be a father to my son." *Poke, poke—jab!*

Karyn reached for the half-empty prescription bottle, held it tightly in her hand.

No one could comprehend how lonely she felt lately, even in a crowded room. And that Zane fellow, what exactly was his deal? How dare he suggest she was choosing not to live!

Of course, she wanted to live a full life. She'd fought hard to keep from drowning in the wake of her sorrow after losing Dean. It took everything she had to continue paddling water now, after Grayson broke her heart.

On the outside, she looked put together. On the inside, she was dying.

She removed the lid on the bottle, shook two tablets into the palm of her hand. Before she could change her mind, she popped the pills into her mouth and swallowed.

Soon—the lost feeling would pass. In addition to relieving the throbbing that still plagued her ankle, she knew the drug would dilute the anger that broiled in her gut.

She wanted to support her family and friends, show them how much they meant to her. But wouldn't it be nice if her tokens of appreciation could be instigated by her genuine desire to show them love, free of obligation and manipulation?

Karyn closed her eyes, leaned back against her sofa.

No one understood how exhausting it was to be this nice, this accommodating. Her entire life had been one long, pleasing festival—always doing what was expected, afraid to rock any boats. Did she even know how to say no? Had there ever been a time when she'd put her needs above others? Frankly, molding herself to meet these heavy obligations left her tired.

So very, very tired . . .

~

KARYN WASN'T sure how long she'd been asleep when a knock at the door woke her. Groggy, she pulled herself up and hobbled to the door. "Hold on, I'm coming," she barked, not bothering to hide her irritation.

She flung the door open, rubbed at the corner of one eye. "Mr. Keppner?"

Zane looked her over. "Ms. Macadam." He held up her empty plate. "Thought it would be polite to return this."

"Huh? Oh, yeah. Thanks." She took the plate from him, waited.

He didn't move to leave. Instead, he studied her. "You okay?" he asked.

Karyn drew a deep breath. "Fine," she told him, a little sharper than necessary. "I was just—uh, I took a nap."

"And I woke you."

She fought to keep from rolling her eyes. At least you couldn't call him stupid.

"Can I come in?"

"Now?"

The deep crinkles at the corner of his eyes deepened. It was as if he was laughing at her without cracking a smile. "If it's convenient, yeah. I'd like to come in."

She wanted to tell him no, it wasn't convenient and she didn't want him to come in. She wasn't at her best. Maybe he could return later, when she wasn't foggy-brained and had on fresh lipstick.

Instead, she pasted a smile just like she always did. Against her better judgment, she stepped back and motioned for him to enter.

"Nice place," he said, after looking around. He pointed to Dean's trophies, which she'd recently put back up. "These your former—"

"Yes, they're Dean's."

What was this guy all about? I mean, he just shows up and wants to chat?

Zane stepped closer, read some of the engravings. He gave a low whistle. "Looks like he was something."

"Oh, he was," she assured him, feeling a bit smug, as if somehow her former husband's accomplishments were her own. "Before his fatal accident, Dean had quite a run, winning consecutive world cup titles and freestyle ski world championship medals. There was no doubt in anyone's mind he'd bring home the gold at the upcoming Olympics."

Zane turned. "And you? What are you good at, Ms. Macadam?"

The question surprised her, made her annoyed. "I'm not sure what you're getting at, but I'm not interested in playing."

He raised his eyebrows. "You think I'm playing a game?" Intensity smoldered in his eyes, so bold she had to look away.

He let her off the hook, strolled over to her bookcase. He pulled a volume into his hands. "So, you're a Hemingway fan?"

Her eyebrows lifted in a challenge of sorts. "You're not?"

He shrugged. "I wouldn't say I'm not a fan, but I find his style a bit—well, over extended. Sadly, many of his more known novels ring hollow for me. That said, I do appreciate his simple, direct and unadorned style."

Karyn pulled her shoulders into a slight shrug. "True, some believe Hemingway's prose is too nostalgic and runs to the sentimental, but I disagree with your take. Hemingway was anything but simple." She wanted to further defend his work, make the point that Hemingway believed the deeper meaning of a story should not be evident on the surface, but should shine through implicitly—a method of writing he termed the *iceberg theory*— but she recalled how Zane had accused her of hiding from life, considered the metaphor and thought better of it. "Literary appraisal aside—as a reader, his work strikes a chord in me. And many others," she couldn't help but add.

"Okay, I can buy off on that." He held up the volume he'd pulled off the shelf. "This one of your favorites?"

She recognized the spine and nodded. "Yes, I loved Farewell to Arms. Have you read it?"

He admitted he had, but it was a long time ago.

"Well, you'll remember the story features Lieutenant Frederic Henry who loves an American nurse deeply, until she rejects him." She gave Zane a sardonic smile. "Let's just say, I relate."

He laughed.

She let herself laugh as well.

He put the book back on the shelf. That's when he saw the prescription bottle on the table.

"What?" she demanded, seeing a look cross his face. "They're for my ankle."

He lifted open palms. "Don't have to get defensive. I'm not the drug police."

Internally, Karyn growled. How could a man be so fascinating —yet so infuriating?

There was no doubt Zane Keppner was intelligent, could be a bit cocky, yet charming. He certainly wasn't afraid to step out of his comfort zone and try new things. Those were the good things. There was a downside. She suspected he could be horribly judgmental. He might phrase it another way, say he was insightful, but he was definitely judgmental.

Yet, he had another aspect that intrigued her. He was as real as rain, didn't do anything out of the need to impress. It was as if he simply didn't care what people thought of him.

"Hey, by chance you have any vanilla ice cream?" he asked her.

She looked at him, confusion crossing her face. "Ice cream?"

"Yeah, you have some in the freezer?" Without waiting for her to answer, he moved into the kitchen, headed for her refrigerator.

"I keep my ice cream in the freezer," she said with a meaningful look, and then grudgingly, "In the garage."

He turned, stared at her with a wide smile on his face. "Well, what are you waiting for? Go get it."

Karyn's eyebrows lifted. "Gee, okay. I guess I will." While Zane remained behind, she retrieved a container of her favorite Tillamook French vanilla ice cream, carried it back into the kitchen and placed it on the counter. "There—will this do?" she said, dryly.

"Perfect." He rubbed the palms of his hands together. "Now, I need some butter, brown sugar and some cream. If you don't have cream, milk will do. Oh, and some vanilla and a little salt." He delivered the list like machine-gun fire.

Curious, she headed for the fridge, pulled out the ingredients and placed them on the counter next to the ice cream. She pointed to the cupboard. "Not sure what you're up to, but the bowls are up there."

Over the next minutes, Zane cooked up homemade caramel

sauce, without bothering to measure any of the ingredients. He simply eyeballed and poured, or tossed in what he thought looked to be the right amount.

She peeked over his shoulder. "I'm not sure I want to feed your—uh, confidence—but that looks delicious."

He grinned. "It is."

He pulled the pan from the stove, announced the sauce was ready. Karyn helped him scoop ice cream into dessert bowls and watched as he poured his creation over the top, in extremely liberal amounts.

"Shhh—don't tell anyone," he said. "But, this is one of my favorites. I eat caramel ice cream sundaes at least three times a week."

"So that's your secret to staying so thin?"

"It's a secret sauce without any calories," he teased, clearly amused. "See?"

Then, in a surprise move, he took her hand, dipped her finger in the bowl, pulling it through the ice cream and sauce. With his eyes holding hers, he brought her finger to his mouth and slowly sucked the sauce off.

"Oh, yeah," he moaned. "Caramel is my absolute favorite."

17

The lobby of the Sun Valley Lodge was quiet this early in the morning. Only a few guests milled around. Most remained in their rooms, some ordering room service and some showering and getting ready to come down to Gretchen's for the eggs benedict special—one of Leigh Ann's personal favorites.

Wanting to make a good first-day impression, she'd pulled herself from her bedsheets while it was still dark outside and climbed in the shower, leaving Mark soundly sleeping. He'd had a bad night, tossing and turning, and she didn't want to wake him.

She knew Karyn usually arrived around seven-thirty. Thanks to the security personnel who were charmed by her relentless claims that she was not only an employee, but family, she was able to spend the time waiting in her sister's office, tidy up for her. "I assure you, Karyn won't mind," she told them.

Karyn's desk was piled with files, mostly related to the upcoming Vanguard conference. Leigh Ann was well aware of the conference and all its trappings. As tourism director, she'd been planning ways to maximize the economic impact to the Sun

Valley area for weeks. Well, before she'd been marched to the door and shown the way out.

Curious, she slipped open a rather large folder and began scanning the contents. The guest list, which would remain secret to the public, was impressive and included some of the most recognizable media celebrities and business owners in America and abroad. There were social media CEOs and presidents of news agencies. There were clothing designers and entertainment industry moguls. The net worth represented in the gathering was staggering and had earned Vanguard the moniker *Summer Camp for Billionaires*.

Moreover, the conference attendees and meeting agenda was held in the utmost confidentiality. While there would be the gaggles of reporters and camera men trying to get the scoop, the Sun Valley Lodge would be closed to the public during the entire conference and security would remain high.

Fascinated by this side of things, Leigh Ann delved in, reading the menu and checking the security plans, the room booking details, pulling her attention away only when she heard a light rap at the door.

Karyn's boss, Jon Sebring, stood in the open doorway. He looked around. "Is—uh, is Karyn here? We have a meeting with the conference director to go over some final details."

Leigh Ann glanced at the wall clock, realized her sister was uncharacteristically late. "She must be running just a little bit late. I'm sure she'll be here soon."

Jon scowled. "The meeting is in five minutes."

"Karyn's been a little under the weather with that ankle and all. Like I said, I'm positive she won't be long." Leigh Ann's mind scrambled to cover for her sister. "I can attend in her stead—until she arrives," she offered.

Jon looked reluctant. "Well, I suppose you could take notes to relay on to your sister."

Leigh Ann held up the file. "Absolutely! I've read everything and I can cover until she can join us." She grabbed a notebook and pen, along with the files she thought were most important, and followed Jon to the Duchin Lounge, a charming wood-paneled bar with a history of serving the best hot buttered rum drinks après-ski to celebrities like Lucille Ball and Gary Cooper.

The conference director, a business magnate from New York who made his fortune in the financial markets, was seated at a table near a window overlooking the ice-skating rink.

Jon introduced her. "Horace, this is Leigh Ann Blackburn. She and Karyn Macadam, who will be joining us shortly, will be your main contacts here at the lodge during the conference. They will be overseeing anything relating to Vanguard and security." Jon turned to Leigh Ann. "This is Horace Mikel, the conference director."

The well-dressed Mr. Mikel stood, extended a hand. "Nice to meet you, Ms. Blackburn."

"Likewise." She smiled, determined to be not only pleasant, but knowledgeable. She couldn't let Karyn down.

Karyn leaned against the plush pillows, briefly glancing at the motorcycle helmet on the bedside table. She couldn't contain her smile as she pulled her attention back to the black curls on the pillow next to her.

Her fingers lightly caressed his broad shoulder, appreciating the heat of his skin.

To her sudden chagrin, the alarm clock buzzed, jolting her rudely awake. Unnerved, she raised one sleepy eyelid and scrambled to turn it off.

A dream?

Shaken, she swept her legs to the floor and sat still for several seconds, trying to get her bearings. The urge to return to the warmth of her bed was strong, as was the desire to escape back into the fantasy she'd dared to dream. It was so unlike her to play out such risqué scenes, to imagine out-of-character interactions with a man she'd barely met. Clearly, his visit had an undeniable impact—at least to her subconscious.

Zane Keppner would be considered a mike drop for most gals. She, on the other hand, had decided it safer to stick with girlfriends for companionship. Better yet, her sisters.

Still, what could a little dream hurt?

Feeling a bit cotton-mouthed, she reached for the glass of water. Finding it empty, she wandered barefoot into the bathroom with the empty tumbler, held it under the faucet.

The image that stared back at her in the mirror was not a pretty picture. There were dark circles under her eyes, flattened hair on one side and sticking out on the other.

She took a long drink of water, then wandered back into the bedroom, glanced at the clock.

Her heart nearly stopped.

What?

Oh, no—NO! She was over an hour late for her meeting!

Karyn looked around the room in confusion. How could she have let this happen?

Her heart raced, sweat broke out on her brow. She scrambled to grab some clothes from the closet. No, not that skirt. She tossed the garment aside, pulled a simple navy sleeveless sheath dress from its hanger and flung it over her head.

She wouldn't have time for a shower. Instead, she raced back to the bathroom, ran a wet wash cloth across her face, her chest, and under her armpits, then dabbed on some antiperspirant. She swiped some gloss on her lips, some mascara on her lashes. Finally, she yanked a brush through that unruly hair and wound it up on her head, clipped the messy bun in place.

Only an idiot would be late for a meeting with Horace Mikel!

Mentally calculating how long it would take her to drive the short distance to the lodge, she grabbed her bag and raced for the door while texting a quick message to Jon telling him she was on the way.

A short time later, she entered the lodge through the side delivery door, knowing it would be faster than the front entrance, raced down the narrow hallway and burst through a backdoor into the Duchin Room, only to find the room empty. A single table was littered with coffee mugs.

Bill appeared from the back room carrying a rack of clean glasses. "If you're looking for Jon and the others, they just left."

Panicked, she thanked him and raced through the lobby toward the reception desk.

"Karyn, there you are!" Her sister waved to her from behind the reception desk, a wide smile plastered on her face. One look at Karyn and Leigh Ann grew concerned. "What's the matter?"

"The meeting, I—"

"Yeah, where were you?" Leigh Ann threw an empty pen into the trash, smiled back at her.

The squeeze in Karyn's chest became a sting in her eyes. She couldn't cry—not here. Not at work. She quietly sniffed and blinked furiously, trying to keep her feelings in check.

"Oh, Karyn—honey! Don't worry about it. I covered for you."

"You what?" Karyn instantly turned furious. "Why would you presume to do that?"

Leigh Ann looked at her as if she had grown a horn out of her forehead. "You weren't here. Jon was concerned and I stepped in, assured him I would take careful notes and pass them on to you." She lifted a sheaf of papers as proof she'd done her self-appointed job.

Ignoring the flush Karyn felt rising on her cheeks, her sister continued. "That Horace Mikel is sure a nice man. He was concerned about security." She paused, held up a file. "But, I assured him the plans were in place and he had nothing to worry about."

Karyn ripped the file from her sister's hand. "Where did you get this?"

Her sister gave her a patient look. "I found it on your desk."

Karyn glanced around, lowered her voice. "Yes, I know it was on my desk. What were you doing in my office?"

Before her sister could answer, Jon appeared, coming from his office down the hall. "Karyn, we missed you this morning."

"Yes, you got my text?"

He nodded. "Under the circumstances, I thought we should go ahead and—"

"Jon, I'm so sorry," she interrupted. "I—well, this ankle keeps me up. I'm afraid I didn't hear the alarm." She should come up with a better excuse, but her mind wouldn't cooperate and be creative.

He smiled. "No worries. Leigh Ann did just fine. I think she developed a nice affinity with Horace and he left the meeting assured all the details for the upcoming Vanguard conference were in order."

He turned to Leigh Ann. "Thanks, again."

Her sister blushed. "No problem. I was glad to help."

Perhaps Leigh Ann was indeed trying to simply be helpful, but Karyn couldn't help but feel annoyed. She'd worried hiring her sister would be a mistake, imagined Leigh Ann's strong character might cause some issues that might require uncomfortable intervention. She'd never expected her sister wouldn't have the common decency not to cross certain boundaries—that she'd horn in on her job responsibilities.

Jon slipped his pen into his inside jacket pocket. "Leigh Ann, I was particularly interested in your idea to hide electrically-charged wire in walls of shrubbery to keep the public, and any aggressive media, from breaching off-limit areas. Secure, yet aesthetically pleasing."

Leigh Ann beamed. "Like I mentioned in the meeting, I've

employed this tactic many times at events. It has proven to be effective."

Karyn could see Jon was impressed. "I have to admit, when Karyn mentioned she was bringing a family member on board, I was a bit reluctant." He placed a hand on Karyn's shoulder, gave a squeeze. "I'm glad I trusted her judgment."

When he was gone, Leigh Ann looked over at Karyn and smiled. "I can see why you love working here. Jon Sebring is amazing." Before Karyn could respond, the phone on the counter rang and Leigh Ann picked up the receiver, answering with a sing-song voice Karyn could barely stomach. "Good morning, Sun Valley Lodge."

Karyn stomped to her office, flung her briefcase on the floor and sunk into her desk chair.

She wanted to be angry with her sister, yet in part, this was all her fault. She'd slept in and missed a very important meeting. Still, she would have hoped Jon might have stalled until she got there. But, no—Take-Over Barbie stepped in and saved the day.

Karyn buried her head in her hands. In the rush, she'd neglected to remember to take a pain pill. Now she was paying for it. Every muscle in her body seemed to ache, even more than her ankle.

By noon, the discomfort had gotten so bad, she picked up the phone. "Leigh Ann, I have an errand to run. I won't be gone long. If anyone is looking for me, don't do *anything*. Simply tell them I'll be back in a half hour."

"Goodness, you're crabby this morning. Did you get enough sleep?"

"Don't push, Leigh Ann," she warned. "You are only going to cover the front desk until I get back. Nothing more," she repeated so they understood each other. She wanted no confusion about that.

"Okay, fine, Go," she said, waving her off. "I've got it."

At home, Karyn rushed into her bathroom only to find the

prescription bottle nearly empty. As if to prove the fact, she turned the tiny container upside down and a single tablet fell onto the counter.

"Okay, don't panic," she told herself, shoving the pill back in and tucking the bottle inside her pocket. Simply call Dr. O'Brien and get a refill.

She pulled her phone from her purse, punched in the number from the list of stored contacts and waited.

"Hello. Dr. O'Brien's office."

"Yes, this is Karyn Macadam. I'm a patient and—"

"Hi, Karyn!" Only then did she recognize the voice of his nurse, her former high school classmate. "Hey, Amber. I'm afraid I've run out of my pain prescription—for my torn ankle ligament —and I was wondering if your office would be willing to call in a refill?"

"Okay, right. Hold a minute and I'll check with the doctor."

Karyn checked her watch as she climbed back in her car and headed back to the office. A chilly breeze blew through the open window, ruffling her hair. She took a deep whiff of the flower-scented air and relaxed into the white leather seat, as she pulled up to the light at Sun Valley Road and slowed, waiting for a chance to turn.

"Karyn?" Amber's voice pulled her from her thoughts.

"Yes, I'm here."

"I'm sorry, but Dr. O'Brien reminded me of the stricter guidelines concerning opioid medications. He can't just call in a refill. I'm afraid you'll have to come in and be seen again before he can issue another fill order."

Karyn thought of arguing for an exception. The Vanguard conference was right around the corner. She couldn't possibly take more time off work.

"I'll try to squeeze you in as soon as possible," Amber offered. "If that helps."

Her mind raced, hoping for an exception. "Thanks, Amber. I

appreciate you checking with the doctor. Unfortunately, my schedule won't allow me to take time off work anytime soon. I'd hoped maybe—"

"Like I said, I wish there was something we could do." Amber's voice took on an apologetic tone. "But well, you understand. Rules are rules. In the meantime, I suggest you treat the discomfort with a little ibuprofen."

Karyn rolled her eyes. This pain could hardly be called discomfort. "Thanks, Amber. I'll call and make that appointment when I get back to the office and can check my calendar."

"Great. We'll get you in as soon as possible," she promised.

Frustrated, Karyn hung up and slipped her phone into her bag, noting her ankle was now swelling. She'd just have to make that pill last, break it in half if necessary. And maybe she could ice her ankle when she got back to the office.

Twenty minutes later she was back at the lodge. Leigh Ann on the phone with a guest. "I'm so glad to hear that. Congratulations on your choice to spend part of your summer in Sun Valley! I have your reservation secured for the Clint Eastwood room for the weeks you requested. I can't wait for you to arrive and see for yourself what a Sun Valley summer is really all about. You'll want to make the most of your time in the Wood River Valley from the moment you arrive—there is so much to do and not a moment to waste. I took the liberty and prepared a three-day suggested itinerary as your guide. Please keep in mind that days are long here, so pace yourself, take time out to just look at the beauty around you, hydrate, and don't worry about missing something—you can always come back!" She waved her fingers in her sister's direction, smiling. "Remember, you can call me anytime should anything come up. We're always here for you."

Karyn cringed. Her sister was perfect for this job, a fact that should make her happy.

"There you are," Leigh Ann said, hanging up the phone.

"Yes, here I am," Karyn said, feeling harried and exhausted. She needed to get this foot up.

Oblivious to Karyn's subdued frame of mind, Leigh Ann rounded the front counter, beaming. "Everything was fairly quiet while you were gone," she reported. "The guests in the Marilyn Monroe room wanted more towels. A family staying in a queen suite wanted moved to a terrace view. And I took seven new reservations." She held up a leather-bound booklet. "These instructions were a little unclear, so I took the liberty to revise them and reprinted a set."

Bristling, Karyn pasted a phony smile and responded. "Great, Leigh Ann. That's just great."

"Oh! Aggie called and said they will be arriving tomorrow. She wanted to make sure you were picking them up at the airport. She and Bert also want to take you to dinner and said for you to make a reservation at—" Her sister paused, checked her notes on the tiny piece of paper in her hand. "Yes, at the Christiana—and to make sure they have a bottle of Muscadet chilling."

Without barely taking time for a breath, Leigh Ann continued to rattle on. "I hope you don't mind, but I took the liberty to research some of our competitors. I created a spreadsheet of promotional activities large hotels at Whistler and Aspen have utilized to successfully promote and grow customer loyalty. Have you set up an Instagram account for the lodge?" she asked.

Sometimes Karyn wondered how Leigh Ann's head didn't explode from all the minutiae she tried to keep track of. No detail was too small for her attention. She micromanaged everything and everyone in her life. And the fact she'd referenced *our* competitors had not slipped by.

Remember, this is just temporary, Karyn reminded herself, and she meant it, whether Leigh Ann comprehended the fact or not.

18

Joie took a deep breath, closed her eyes as what felt like metal pincers squeezed her heart. She got out of the car, looked up and down the wide, tree-lined boulevard, trying with very little luck to push the niggling doubt from her mind.

Of course, she was doing the right thing. What else could she do under these circumstances?

With renewed determination, she marched up the cobblestone sidewalk, climbed the steps to the wide colonial-styled porch and parked herself in front of the shiny black door. Taking another deep breath, she jabbed the doorbell—twice, for good measure.

Despite her steadfast resolve, her hands grew sweaty as she waited, wondering what she would actually say at the first sight of him. Finally, she heard a sound on the other side and the door opened revealing an older woman with graying hair clipped on top of her head wearing a faded Boise State t-shirt and jeans. "Can I help you?" she asked.

Joie looked her over, pulled herself tall. "I need to speak with

Andrew Merrill." She realized her voice came out resembling that of a mean dog, but it didn't matter. "Now."

The woman instinctively took a step back. "I—I'm sorry. Mr. Merrill is at his office today. Mrs. Merrill had errands to run. I'm the housekeeper. Can I take a message?"

Joie took pity on the woman who was unfortunate enough to be in the firing line of her very bad mood. "No, that's okay." She whirled and stomped back to her jeep. With building anger barely in check, she climbed behind the wheel and started the engine, pulled out onto the manicured boulevard with tires squealing.

The firm was located in downtown Boise on the twenty-fourth floor of a high rise located just south of the capitol building with spacious views of the foothills and Table Rock, a plateau overlooking the city that remained a favorite among trail enthusiasts. Joie couldn't help but remember sitting in a car with Andrew parked on the overlook near the well-known lighted cross erected by the Jaycees. They'd nearly been discovered in a state of undress by a scout troop hunting for arrowheads.

She shook her head, angrily. How could she have been so stupid to believe succumbing to an insistent married man would end well? Not only had she violated the message of that cross, but she'd made herself the target of a lot of pain. Like Father John warned in his Sunday messages, sin ripples, sending waves of destruction into the lives around you.

Boy, had this situation proved that adage to be true.

Joie strode through massive glass doors and across the shiny lobby floor to the bank of elevators and punched the button, waited. Not so long ago, she'd been a first year associate standing at this very spot, looking forward to a bright career unmarred by her poor choices. A lifetime had passed since then.

The elevator dinged, the doors opened and out stepped two guys she recognized from the financial investment company located in the building. They recognized her as well and nodded.

She stepped inside the empty elevator and quickly pressed the button to the twenty-fourth floor. The doors slid shut and she rode alone with only her thoughts to keep her company.

Joie could often be accused of flying by the seat of her pants, and in this situation, her accusers would not be far off. Sure, she'd had a plan—a plan that quickly flew out the window when she found Andrew not at home. But she wasn't about to return to Sun Valley without a confrontation.

Just who did he think he was, using the legal system to gain shared custody of a baby he had never wanted in the first place? He'd even thrown out the idea of an appointment to rid them of the *problem*. Well, she was not about to allow that creep anyway near Hudson. Not now, not ever!

The elevator chugged to a stop. The doors opened to the familiar lobby, with its glossy tiles laid in a pattern that included the firm's logo. The reception desk erupted from the center of the room with a ceiling so tall, voices lightly echoed in competition with the jazz tunes pumped from carefully disguised speakers.

"Joie Abbott? Well, it's nice to see you again." The receptionist, whose name she couldn't recall right now, smiled widely. "What can I do for you?"

She found herself wishing she'd worn a skirt and pumps. "I'm here to see Andrew Merrill."

"Sure." The receptionist lifted the phone receiver, held it to her ear. "Do you have an appointment?"

Joie shook her head.

"No worries," the receptionist winked. "I'll let him know you're here."

Minutes later, he appeared in his standard suit and tie, not a strand of his jet-black hair out of place. "Joie, you shouldn't be here."

She swallowed her fury, lowered her voice. "You think I'm going to—"

He grabbed her arm. "Let's take this to my office." He looked at the surprised receptionist. "I'm not to be interrupted."

Andrew nearly flung her inside his corner office, closed the door behind them. "You should know better than anyone how inappropriate this is."

Joie could stand it no longer. She laughed bitterly. "Inappropriate? Oh, that's classic!" She nearly spit the words out.

"Settle down, or I'll call security," he warned.

Joie took a menacing step forward. "No amount of security is going to keep me from fighting you. He's *my* son—not yours."

"Perhaps I need to remind you that I—"

She jabbed her finger in the air. "No! A night or two of jiffy-stiffing does not entitle you to my baby, a baby you never wanted, a baby you've never even seen!" She dug in her bag and retrieved a copy of the document he'd signed. "Besides all that, you signed any rights you had away." She tossed the stapled papers at his feet.

Andrew's cognac-colored eyes grew steely. "I agree that document can be a very challenging hurdle to reverse, but I have every reason to believe the court will side with me and my wife."

Joie suddenly remembered the housekeeper's reference to a wife, a fact she'd failed to initially clue into because of her nerves. "So, let me guess," she said with sarcasm. "You married Paralegal Wendy and she wants to play mommy? Tell her to go have her own baby."

He broke gaze, smirked. "You hadn't heard? I've reconciled with Victoria."

Joie rolled her eyes. "Oh, lucky her!"

"She and I believe—"

"How cozy. You even talk to her now? Tell me, what did you ever say to convince her to overlook your many and often-repeated indiscretions?" Joie wished she could erase her own name from that list. "What lie did you tell her to make her believe you could ever be trusted?"

"My marriage is not the issue here."

She squared her shoulders. "You're right. The issue is you need to drop this farce, and drop it now!"

He moved to his desk, had the nerve to casually lean against the corner before responding. "I'm afraid I can't."

It took every ounce of self-restraint she could muster not to slap that pretty man-face. "And why not?" she demanded.

"Initially, I offered you the option to terminate this pregnancy," he reminded her in a voice that cut like a knife. "If you had, I wouldn't be forced into this position."

"He's not your son!" she screamed, not caring who heard through the walls.

"I think the courts might disagree."

Joie could barely breathe. "Why? What reason could you possibly have for wanting to be in this baby's life? You just admitted you didn't want him." It dawned on her then—the truth. "Oh, I get it. Victoria wants this baby."

Andrew slowly nodded. "Yes. My wife wants a family. After everything I've put her through, the least I can do is give her that."

"You are using my son as a pawn to restore your marriage? That's gut-belly low—even for you. Besides, why can't you just—"

"She can't."

Reality hit Joie hard. She stumbled back with the impact. "I don't care what you say, the court will never agree. You signed away your rights."

Even as the words left her mouth, she knew Andrew had connections in the legal community that were far-reaching. He'd been on several judicial selection committees, golfed with many of those sitting on the judiciary. Sure, they would claim no bias— but anyone with a lick of sense knew he'd launch a vigorous attempt to reinstate his rights with a parade of affidavits pointing out her past, the drinking and wild living. No doubt, he wouldn't stop until he'd shredded her.

Andrew could have a real shot at gaining shared custody, especially with Victoria by his side, a highly-respected local business woman from a family with their own connections.

A dismal future flashed through Joie's mind. She saw Christmas trees with un-opened presents, family Thanksgiving dinners with empty chairs next to her own—month-long summer vacations with her little boy in Boise, or on a European trip with Andrew and his wife.

She groaned inside, tried to keep her hands from shaking. This man had the power to destroy her and she knew he would wield that power—whatever it took.

For the first time, she knew pure terror.

19

It was another perfect sunny day when Leigh Anne woke up the next morning. The weather was warm, and the sky was a brilliant blue. Mark came downstairs before she did, and had already made bacon to go with poached eggs and toast. He was pouring the water into their Keurig when Leigh Anne walked into the kitchen.

"Smells delicious," she said, as he handed her a mug of steaming French roast. He pressed the lever on the coffee maker and waited for the machine to brew his cup. A moment later, he set her breakfast plate down on the table for her.

"Thank you for making breakfast," she said politely as he sat down across from her, with his own plate of bacon and eggs. Frankly, this was a huge surprise. She couldn't remember the last time Mark made breakfast, or did any chores around the house for that matter. Could this be a sign he was getting finally over his slump?

Mark placed a linen napkin across his lap. "So, how'd it go at the Sun Valley Lodge?"

His question took her back some. Initially, he'd seemed reluctant, even resentful, that she would consider working for her sister. Not that he had a choice. Neither of them did. The earnings, though small, would help their dire cash flow situation. They needed the money.

"Well, I really enjoyed it." She told him about filling in for Karyn when she missed the meeting. In the past, anything related to the annual Vanguard meeting would pique his interest. She knew her husband longed to be in that financial stratosphere—where the big boys ran. His words—not hers.

Surprisingly, he asked nothing. "I'm glad, honey. You're really good at that kind of stuff." She could see a moment of fleeting pain cross his face, knew he was sorry she'd lost her position at the tourism council and blamed himself. "What was up with your sister? It's not like her to miss a meeting like that."

"I know. I'm really concerned about her. She seems to have gone adrift again, just like after Dean died, or maybe worse."

"Worse?"

"Yeah, it's as if she is angry with the entire world. She certainly wasn't happy with me or any of my suggestions."

"Well, babe—you do tend to take things over."

Leigh Ann huffed and gave him a dirty look. "I do not," she argued. Why did everyone always accuse her of taking over, of controlling, when all she was trying to do was help? Could she help it if God created her smart and organized? It was a gift, and shame on anyone who tried to diminish those abilities just because they compared their own skills and felt inadequate?

Mark held up his hands. "Look, I'm not trying to start a fight. I'm simply suggesting that Karyn may feel a little threatened."

Leigh Ann hadn't considered that possibility, but Mark was right. She could see that now. The look on Karyn's face when Jon complimented her said it all.

"I suppose you're right," she told her husband, while reaching for the salt shaker. "She's going through a hard time adjusting to Grayson leaving. I suppose I could back off and give her a little more room to shine without standing in my shadow."

Mark scooped up his toast, took a bite. "That's my girl," he said, chewing.

Leigh Ann scowled. "I know it's just us, but it's impolite to talk and eat at the same time."

He tossed his toast onto his plate. "Why do you do that?"

"What?"

"Why must you always criticize? We were having a nice morning. Did you have to act like my mother and give me a lesson in table manners?"

She glared back at him. "I wouldn't have to act like your mother if you would remember you're not some animal roaming up to the dining table with your hairy chest hanging out of your robe. Would it have hurt for you to put on some clothes?"

"I didn't want to risk waking you! In fact, I snuck down and let you sleep so I could surprise you with breakfast." He pulled the napkin from his lap, threw it to the table. "Shame on me for being considerate."

Leigh Ann realized she'd taken the argument too far, reached for his arm. "Mark, don't. I'm sorry. I don't want to fight. I appreciate you cooking breakfast. I do."

Mark gave her a tentative look, like he was considering his options. Finally, he sat. "Look, I'm sorry too. This mess we're in— it's all my fault."

"Mark, don't—"

He shook his head. "No. It is. We've both been under tremendous strain. We're both short-tempered because of all that's been hitting us. But, I have some good news."

Her heart skipped. "You got a job?"

"No. But I've got to tell you something—and it's important."

She placed her fork on the table, no longer hungry. "Is this about all the incidents we've been having? Are we in more danger than everyone's been telling us?"

He quickly reached for her hand. "No—well, yes. They caught the perpetrator."

Relief rushed through her. "They did? Who?"

Mark's face grew even more serious, if that was possible. "Buck Randles."

Leigh Ann's hand went to her chest. "The school janitor? But we know him! Why would Mr. Randles do such a thing?' Even as the words left her mouth, she knew the answer to her question. "Oh."

Mark nodded. "Seems he lost some retirement funds in the Preston deal."

Still, she couldn't believe such a benign old man could have instigated such acts of retribution. "He torched my roses!" she said. "But he's a grandfather. What's the matter with people?"

Mark squeezed her hand. "Honey, there's more. What I have to tell you is extremely confidential. I mean it. You can't share this with your dad, your sisters—not with anyone. I'm putting myself at risk even telling you. But I can't keep secrets—not anymore." He took a deep breath. "Remember my meeting with Reece Rusk at the Pioneer Saloon?"

"Yes. I thought you said he didn't offer you a job?" she asked, confused.

Mark nodded. "I didn't tell you the rest." He explained how he'd been surprised when two other men joined them for lunch —one the general counsel for Rusk's company, the other an FBI agent.

"An FBI agent?" She pulled her hand from her husband's. "Oh Mark, what have you done?"

He quickly assured her he was not the target. "Well, not really. But they are investigating Andrea."

"Your business partner?"

"Former business partner," he reminded. "Apparently, she was not everything I understood her to be."

When Mark finished telling his story, she shook her head. "I don't like this, Mark. It sounds dangerous. Besides, we're already in hot water with everyone we know, except my family. What if something goes wrong? What if—"

"I don't have a choice," he warned her.

She stood, paced the kitchen. "Of course you have a choice. They can't force you to play this cops and robbers game. Our lives are not some television drama."

"I don't have a choice," he repeated. "If I don't help them, they will try and implicate me as well."

"But you didn't do anything?" She could tell her question— her doubt—hurt him.

"No," he quickly assured her. "I didn't. At least, not knowingly."

"What are you saying?"

He got up and came to her, drew her into a tight hug. "I got in over my head this time, Leigh Ann. Seems she's a player, and it's very possible she played me as well."

Before she could respond to that, her cell phone rang. She pulled away from Mark's embrace and headed for the table, picked it up. "It's Colby!" she said. "He wants to Facetime."

She quickly ran her hand through her hair and pressed accept. The tiny screen erupted with her precious son's face. "Colby?"

"Hi, Mom!"

Mark squeezed in next to her. "Son? It's good to hear from you."

"Hi, Dad—good to see you guys. I miss you."

Leigh Ann searched her son's face. "Are you eating? Sleeping?"

Colby chuckled. "Uh, yeah. Check all the boxes. I'm fine. Look, I don't have much time and I wanted to talk to you guys before Nicole wakes. I have news."

Mark and Leigh Ann exchanged worried glances.

"News?" Leigh Ann asked, feeling her throat constrict. "What kind of news?"

"Nothing bad," he told them. "It's just that—well, they're moving me."

Mark ran his hand through his uncombed hair, not bothering to hide his concern. "Where to, Son?"

"The border of Syria. While I can't share details, it seems there is some building tension, and they want more troops in the area. Just a precaution."

Leigh Ann's fingers trembled as she fought to hold the phone steady. First came Mark's news about the FBI investigation. Now Colby's frightening announcement.

With her free hand, she fingered the pendant her son had given her, slid it back and forth on its chain. On the turn of a dime, it seemed her entire life had turned into a war zone.

20

An ominous, unspecific feeling of dread followed Karyn as she headed for the parking lot and climbed in her car. The last thing she had time for today was leaving work early in order to pick up Bert and Aggie from the airport. The Vanguard conference was only two days away and many of those planning on attending were already showing up with their families, hoping for a few days of relaxing in the high mountains of Idaho before getting down to work.

The airport was bound to be busy. And traffic—well, she knew the roads would be clogged with traffic. Whenever celebrities descended on Sun Valley, so did over-ambitious media seeking their next scoop and curious tourists wanting a peek into the lives of the rich and famous.

She maneuvered her car onto Sun Valley Road and drove in the direction of Ketchum, past pastoral green pastures filled with horses. Bicyclists made their way along a path bordering the fence line, many of them entire families out getting exercise and enjoying the late afternoon sun. The sight used to make her happy, now—not so much.

She was in a mood, and she admitted the fact. Truth be told, this mood had developed weeks ago and she couldn't seem to shake it. It was totally out of character for her to be this cranky.

There was a time not so long ago when she'd felt invincible. Love does that. It makes you feel infinite and invincible, like the whole world is open to you, anything is achievable, and each day will be filled with wonder.

Karyn pulled to a stop at the light at Main, pondering the fact that when Grayson left, so did her confidence, her belief that everything would indeed turn out okay. She knew now there were no promises in life. Happiness, it seemed, was a crapshoot. She'd rolled the dice twice, put everything on the line for love, and lost —both times.

Sure, she still had her job, but even that couldn't fill the deep hole inside her. She wondered now if the empty pit inside her might ever be filled. Could she climb out of this emotional pit she was mired in and be truly happy again? And not just the happy disposition everyone expected of her, but would she ever feel excited about what was ahead—her future?

When the light turned green, she swung the car onto Main and headed south toward the airport, knowing it would be easy to launch into one of her could-have, should-haves. But that was the problem with attempting to fashion yourself from another person and circumstances outside oneself—the work was never done. Just when you thought you were through, life kicked you in the gut and pulled you back for another round.

For example, spending time with Bert and Aggie Macadam would only marinate her misery and remind her of Dean. While she'd come to an understanding with her former in-laws about her moving on, both in her personal life and in her love life, they would no doubt be happy to learn Grayson was no longer a part of her life. She would remain the wife of only one—their son. At least for now.

That thought pulled her under again. She reached into her bag with her free hand, pulled the prescription bottle and held it in her hand unopened. One pill remained. Admittedly, she no longer needed to take medication to alleviate the ache if she was careful not to remain on her ankle for long periods. The icing option had indeed helped with the swelling.

Karyn pulled off the main highway onto the road leading to the community airport, making her way through a residential area lined with modest homes and box elder trees with their furrowed trunks and yellowish tassels hanging from the limbs—the kind of neighborhood where children played in the front yards unsupervised.

As she neared the entrance gate, she could see Lear jets lined up behind gated sections of the tarmac. In the coming days, security officers would be posted at the entry points for added security during the Vanguard conference. Anyone passing into the area would be required to show credentials.

The Friedman Memorial Airport had been in existence since shortly after the Wright brothers flew the first manned aircraft over one hundred years ago. The current terminal had recently been renovated with raw wood beams overhead and walls of honey-hued logs. A fireplace made of river rock anchored a cozy seating area with windows overlooking the sagebrush covered foothills to the west.

Karyn did her best to push back memories of a day spent with Grayson in the hangars to the east, the impromptu picnic they'd shared and the hours he'd spent introducing her to flying the backcountry. It'd been a marvelous day, one she'd never experience again.

"Yoo-hoo! Karyn, here we are."

She looked in the direction of the familiar voice. Aggie stood by the tiny baggage area, waving. She was wearing tweed slacks and a crisp white sleeveless blouse. Thick, gold jewelry draped her neck and wrists. Bert stood by her side in chinos and a sweater tied over his shoulders. They were exquisitely tanned and looked just as one would expect a person might look after having spent two months cruising the Aegean Sea on a yacht.

"Baby, oh baby—come here," Aggie said, pulling her into a tight hug. "We just heard."

Bert patted her shoulder. "That chap doesn't know what he left behind."

Karyn cringed and gave the clerk at the ticket counter a dirty look. Apparently, the Dilworth sisters weren't the only ones who knew how to spread gossip.

Aggie held Karyn at arm's length, looked her over. "I hate that he broke your heart." She leaned close. "Truth was, I sensed from the very beginning that one couldn't be trusted. There was something in his eyes."

Panic rose in Karyn's throat. She wasn't up to doing this right now—and most certainly not with Dean's parents. "Uh, could you both excuse me? I'm afraid I need to visit the restroom before we head out. Traffic was awful, and well—" She pointed to the restroom and gave an apologetic smile.

"Oh, certainly sweetheart," Aggie said, waving her off. "Go." She placed her manicured hand on Bert's arm. "Honey, get the suitcases, will you?" She turned to Karyn. "We'll meet you outside."

Karyn rushed to the bathroom, made her way to one of two empty stalls. She quickly slid the lever on the door closed, fighting angry tears.

She hadn't wanted to come, didn't have the time. She didn't want to walk through the terminal remembering Grayson's plane was no longer parked outside. She didn't want to be the butt of gossip, and didn't want to give Aggie the pleasure of knowing the relationship she'd argued for had pancaked.

With a groan, she pulled the prescription bottle from her purse, opened it and swallowed that final pill—that tiny bit of escape wrapped in a little white tablet. The promised relief couldn't come fast enough.

Minutes later, she made her way through the terminal, to the entrance where her in-laws waited.

"There you are!" Aggie exclaimed. "We thought you'd gotten lost in there." She laughed at her own simple joke that really wasn't funny at all.

"C'mon, let's get these suitcases loaded," Bert said. He waved a twenty dollar bill at a young guy in a blue shirt with a tag that read *Maintenance*. "Young man, could we get some help with our bags?"

Before Karyn could explain the airport didn't offer concierge service, the kid nodded and grabbed the luggage handles. "Where to?" he asked. At the car, he refused to take Bert's money.

"Take it, son," Bert urged, pressing the bill into his hand.

The young worker shook his head, handed the twenty back. "Nah, it's all right." He gave Karyn a smile.

In the car, Aggie pulled out a hand mirror and fussed with her hair. "I'm going to have to make an appointment at Vertu right away. The downside of traveling abroad is there are no hair stylists that speak your language."

Karyn thrust the car in gear and headed through the neighborhood road. "That was one nice thing about traveling the international ski circuit with Dean. Often, I could just pull on a cute winter knit hat."

Tears immediately welled in Aggie's eyes. "Ah, yes. You two were such a sweet couple. I've never seen a more beautiful bride. Our son loved you so." She shook her head in sadness. "I know you cared for that fellow from Alaska, but he never looked at you the way Dean did. I'm not sure anyone will love you like that."

"Agatha—" Bert interrupted from the back seat, his tone chastising. "You don't know that's true."

Aggie slapped her mirror shut. "Oh, I know it isn't politically correct to say so. But it's true. We all know it."

Frustrated, Karyn gunned the engine. Was Dean's mother right? Had she used up all her happy? Would she shuffle through relationships, never finding anyone who would cherish her the way Dean had?

Thank goodness she'd taken the edge off with that pill, or—

Suddenly, a flash of color in the road. A small boy running after his ball. Karyn screamed, slammed on her brakes.

But, it was too late.

21

J oie leaned and brushed her cheek against Hudson's downy head. She loved the way he smelled, loved to watch him sleep. At times like this, she could almost believe there was nothing sinister looming, no one threatening to take him away.

She hummed a few stanzas of a favorite lullaby and carried him to his cradle, laid him down. The trip to Boise had put her behind. Hours of research loomed ahead for a brief that was due, a situation that promised she would get no sleep until the wee hours of morning. Still, she couldn't bear to walk away. Instead, she patted his little bottom softly and gazed at her sleeping child with tears of frustration streaming down her face.

The doorbell rang, forcing her attention away. Reluctantly, she moved for the front door, opened it. Clint stood on her front porch, two large pizza boxes in his hands. She quickly blinked away her remaining tears. "Clint."

"Hey, hope you like pepperoni," he said, smiling against a backdrop of black sky dotted with stars.

She shuffled, nervously ran her hand through the strands of

her hair. "I know. Yeah. Could we, uh—I need to—I'm sorry. I need to reschedule our dinner."

There was no mistaking the look of disappointment on his face. "Oh, sure."

"Yeah, I'm just really tired."

"Okay."

She felt like a heel, especially after all he'd done for her. "So, I'm sorry you got all dressed up."

He shrugged. "That's okay. It's good for me to put on something other than jeans and boots every once in a while. Reminds me why I'm not an accountant." He looked at her with concern. "Everything okay?"

"What?"

"Are you okay?" he repeated. "Because you don't look okay."

Joie focused on the bear tattoo peeking out from his crisp rolled shirt sleeve. "Well, geez, take me now, sailor."

"I mean, you look distracted."

She took a deep breath. "Distracted, no. Well, maybe—yeah. Distracted, okay, sure. I'm very distracted."

She stepped back, invited him in. Taking the pizza boxes, she slid them onto the counter. "I think I did something really stupid today." She stared at the floor. "I likely made a real mess of things. Tomorrow, I have to tell Maddy that no matter how often she's supported me, I failed to trust her and took things in my own hands. Worse, I've let down my son."

Clint led her to the sofa, motioned for her to sit with him. "Anything I can do?"

Joie couldn't help it. The tears came again. She looked up at Clint miserably. "You know, there are very few times in my life when I find myself sitting around thinking, "I wish I wasn't single," but today, I mean—" She sniffed, rubbed her arm against her nose, feeling her wall of defenses crumble. "I'm happy. You know? I like my life. I like my friends, my family. I like my stuff. I adore my baby boy."

Clint nodded.

"But every now and then, just for a moment, I wish I had a partner, someone to pick up the slack. Someone to wait for the cable guy, make me coffee in the morning, fight the battles that are too damn big for me to fight alone." She let her head drop against her friend's shoulder, let the tears flow freely.

Clint placed his arm around her. "What happened?"

She confided in him, told him about her impromptu trip to Boise and how the confrontation with Andrew had ended. Just like she'd so often seen him do in the courtroom, he'd gone in for the kill.

"You and I both know what the successful practice of law demands," Andrew reminded, as she'd headed for the door. "Choosing to bifurcate your time between your professional and personal life may work if you are a pharmacist—but not in this competitive environment. Is that fair to our son? At least Victoria won't shuffle him off to caretakers."

Andrew intended to break her, even if he didn't out-and-out say so. He knew too much, could easily twist her weaknesses and use them against her.

She'd thought she could pull off this motherhood thing. Just like every other time she'd determined to do life differently, the desire to be better slipped through her fingers because she simply couldn't keep a grip on her impulses. Her life wasn't some feel-good novel where the heroine always faced down danger and won. No super-woman cape hung in her closet.

The truth was, she was just a bright girl who kept swallowing a bunch of stupid—a girl who continually ruined everything.

"I thought I had everything under control," she tried to explain, her voice breaking. "But I don't. I'm failing."

Clint lifted a damp strand of hair from her face and listened quietly.

"I thought I could return to work and take Hudson with me. Instead, I'm having to rely on my sisters, my dad—on you—to help. My work competes with my time with my kid. Something is always having to give. I'm constantly letting down one or the other. And now, Andrew is going to use all that against me to take Hudson away. That's how pathetic I am."

She buried her head in his chest, cried through muffled sobs. "I don't know what to do. I don't know what to do."

Clint hugged her close, stroked her hair and gently rubbed her arm. "You are not failing." He kissed the top of her head. "Shhh . . . I'm here. And, everything is going to be okay."

22

Leigh Ann jabbed the off button and slammed her phone into her purse. Trembling, she hollered into her husband's office. "Mark! That was dad. There's been an accident. We need to go!" She grabbed her keys from the hook on the wall. "C'mon!"

Mark scrambled and followed her into the garage. "What happened?"

"Karyn. She was picking up Bert and Aggie at the airport and something about a child darting into the street chasing a ball," she reported, feeling frantic inside.

"Oh no! Anybody hurt?" He climbed in the passenger side and closed the door.

Leigh Ann pressed the garage door opener clipped to her visor "No major injuries, thankfully. Including the little boy. The Macadams are still being checked over. They were shaken up, of course. The kid's ball—well, it didn't fare so well." She started the engine, glanced in her rearview mirror and backed out. "Oh, Mark. What if she'd hit that little boy?"

The drive to the hospital seemed to take forever. Even though her sister had been reported unharmed, Leigh Ann needed to see for herself—to hug her and assure her mind Karyn really was okay.

In the car, Mark turned on the radio and dialed into some ridiculous talk show about politics and how the upcoming elections would affect interest rates. "Mark, please," she said, reaching for the radio knob. "Not now." She turned the distracting noise off.

Inside the bright white hospital, Leigh Ann forged ahead straight past the smiling woman at the front desk and headed directly toward the emergency department.

The waiting room was crowded. Her dad was there, of course. So was his ranch manager, Sebastian. Joie walked the floor, patting little Hudson's back. Her friend, Clint, stood by the wall with his hands buried in his pockets. Somehow, they'd all beaten her to the hospital.

"Where is she?" Leigh Ann demanded, trying to manage what she knew were irrational emotions. She'd been told Karyn wasn't hurt.

Mark stood behind her, placed his hands on her shoulders. "Honey, I'm sure—"

"Where is Karyn?" she repeated, flinging off his arms. "I need to see her."

Her dad jumped up from his seat, moved to her side. "She's okay, Leigh Ann. I saw her. She's fine."

As if to punctuate his statement, Karyn appeared from the hallway. The skin under her eyes was blackened with bruising and she had a bandage on her forehead.

Leigh Ann rushed to meet her. "What is all this? I thought you were okay." She looked into her sister's eyes, saw how breakable she was, how fragile. "Oh, honey—come here." She pulled Karyn to herself and hugged tight, as if to send an unspoken message that her older sister was here and now everything would be all right.

Her dad folded his arms around them both as reinforcement

of the same message. Joie joined and leaned her head against the entire bunch.

Karyn lifted her head and pulled back. "I'm fine. Really, I am. Those airbags carry quite the punch is all." She attempted a weak smile.

Finally, Leigh Ann could breathe. "What happened?" she asked, at the same time the Dilworth sisters pressed through the sliding doors that led to the ambulance loading area, followed by Rory Sparks, the town cop.

"Oh, my! We just heard," Miss Trudy announced, deep concern written all over her face.

Ruby shook her head. "Nash down at the coffee shop said Rory got the call right in the middle of eating his cinnamon roll. Everyone in town is worried to death."

Karyn held up open palms, gave them all another weary look. "I'm fine. We're all fine." Saying the statement again seemed to steady her. "That little boy darted out of nowhere."

"Yeah, a close call." Rory held out a clipboard with a sheet of paper and a pen. "You'll have to sign this accident report, Karyn. The damage to your car was fairly minor, given you hit a tree. We had it towed to Greene's."

Her father placed his flannelled arm around her shoulder, gave her a squeeze. "The good Lord was with you today, that's for certain. The little guy fell before landing in the path of your oncoming car. You hit his ball before veering into the tree. A scary situation, but—" His own face filled with emotion. "There was no tragedy." He fingered the tiny bandage on his daughter's forehead. "Bumps heal," he said softly, his eyes moist.

"That's right," Mark said. He nodded toward an open doorway leading to a room lined with curtained patient areas. "Where's Bert and Aggie?"

As if on cue, a nurse appeared leading the older couple out to the waiting room. Behind them walked a man. He pulled a blue-colored cap off his head, revealing a shock of black hair. He followed them out to the waiting room, cleared his throat. "Well, from what I hear, you all were very lucky today."

Karyn's gaze dropped to the floor. Despite the favorable report, Leigh Ann noticed her sister's lip trembled.

"The good news is that I get to go golfing this afternoon after all." He tapped the clipboard in this hand. "The tests I ran show no significant injuries. A little rest and these two lovebirds can go dancing if they so choose."

Bert gave his wife a wink, hugged her shoulder. "Well, maybe we'll settle for watching some television."

Everyone laughed.

It was then that Leigh Ann noticed someone she hadn't seen earlier. That food photographer—what was his name? Zane Keppner. Yes, that was his name.

He sat quietly in a chair next to an aquarium filled with multi-colored fish, leaned forward with his forearms casually resting on his knees and watched the scene that was playing out in the waiting room with a look of reserved fascination.

ZANE TAPPED his thumb against the steering wheel as the car came to a stop in Karyn's driveway. He turned off the engine, looked over at her with a slight grin. "I thought I was going to have to arm wrestle your family members for the privilege of driving you home."

"Yes, thank you. I don't think—I mean, I wasn't up for—" She found herself too choked up to say anything more. Instead, she looked out the window to hide the fact her eyes had filled with tears.

His hand quickly covered hers. "Hey now, what's with the crocodile water?"

She chewed her knuckle, shook her head. "Nothing. It's nothing."

"Those tears tell a different story. Want to talk about it? I've got a good ear."

She sensed he didn't want to overstep his bounds with her, wanted to respect her need for privacy. Even so, her new friend would be shocked to learn the truth, how deep the wound really was. "You don't understand."

"I might. If you want to explain."

She looked at him, weighed her options, knowing that the secret she kept inside had the ability to destroy her if she didn't unburden her soul. "The cop is a friend from high school," she ventured, her voice low and shaky. "He didn't take a blood test."

"And, if he had?"

"I'd likely be in handcuffs." She tasted the sour truth of the statement on her tongue as she said it.

Zane slowly nodded. "You want to tell me about it?"

Karyn let out a nervous laugh. "Do I *want* to? Ha, no. Not especially."

"Yet, you did."

She couldn't argue that. "Yes." She reached for the door handle, glanced back at him. "Are you coming in?"

"Uh, yeah. I'm coming in."

Zane followed her up the sidewalk, quietly stood beside her on the porch as she unlocked her front door. "Can I get you something to drink?" she asked, when the door finally opened and they stepped inside. She tossed the hospital paperwork on the entry table. "Jack Daniels, perhaps?"

"As tempting as that sounds, I think I'd best stick with iced tea." He headed for the sofa as she made her way to the adjoining kitchen. She went for the cupboard where she pulled two tall glasses from the shelf and set them on the counter.

A few short minutes later, she joined him at the sofa, drinks in hand—and feeling as though the weight of the world was on her shoulders. She sank down beside him, reached in her pocket and pulled out the empty prescription bottle. "My ankle—it hurt." She pointed to her walking cast as if to emphasize the fact she had a legitimate injury.

She closed her eyes, shook her head. "No, that's not the entire truth." The admission felt like a stone wedged in her throat. She had no option now but to swallow, or she'd never be able to breathe. "The pills—they took, well they took the edge off."

"The world can be a sharp place." He said it without judgment, like one who had battled his own demons and won.

Karyn glanced around at the familiar walls that often now felt foreign. At times, it was if she was a stranger in her own home. Her fingers trembled as she placed her glass on the coffee table, knowing she had to unload—or implode. "He's out there in Alaska, doing what he always dreamed of. He wakes up and makes his way into a crib and pulls a little person from the rumpled bedding and cuddles him. He's a dad. And I'm happy for him. But there's this other feeling that doesn't feel right, or fair or good."

She fisted her hands, felt her nails dig into the skin of her palms. "I wake up and look over at the other side of the bed, at an empty spot that keeps getting vacated. It's not fair. And I'm angry," she said with tears in her eyes, and then felt silly about it, and embarrassed. Angry wasn't a pretty emotion.

"Grayson is happy—without me. There's this deep pit inside me and I wonder—" She released a gravid sigh, one signaling she was ready to birth unvarnished reality. "The truth is, I wonder if my dreams are over. Maybe I had my dreams, and they're over now. And I'm going to be this single woman, no husband, no kids, no family of my own. I love my dad, my sisters—but it's not the same."

She looked at the ceiling. "They were—well, the rest of me. First, Dean—then Grayson, who by the way, promised he'd love me forever. And I let him go. I didn't even fight. Because I'm too stinking nice. And I always do what is expected, what is best for everyone else."

Karyn stood, paced the floor. "You know he saved me. You weren't here, but you should have seen how I was. I was—dark. Losing Dean made me feel dark inside. Grayson came into my life, and somehow he lit me up."

She stopped, looked at Zane. "I let him go. And it's better—for him. But for me—" Her voice faded. "I need a reason not to take these pills."

"I guess this is where I'm supposed to come up with some wisdom, wax philosophical and provide you another way to view this laceration." He shook his head. "Sorry, I'm not that poetic, except to say this—love doesn't conquer all. It conquers some stuff, but the real problem kicks the ever living crap out of love. Or the loss of it."

She frowned. "The real problem?"

He stood, took her by the shoulders. "Yeah—let's look at what's really going on. The problem isn't them—it's you." He placed his hand over her heart. "There's a hole inside, and no man is ever going to fill it. Neither will the best house in the neighborhood, the perfect job, or a backyard filled with laughing children." He lifted her hand holding the empty prescription bottle. "Or these.

Zane took a step back, looked at her with an intensity that made her cringe under the mass of it. "Mistakes are painful," he told her. "But they're the only way to find out who we really are."

She scowled. "And who I am is just a woman with a hole inside?"

"Don't make light of it. I think you walk into a room, look in other people's eyes to see how you are supposed to feel, how you're supposed to act. If you think someone is unhappy with you, it feels like death." He shrugged. "We're all stupid and just want to be loved. But first, you have to learn to love yourself." His eyes seemed to take on the glint of a politician at a rally. "Remember, I've done the rehab thing. More importantly, that experience helped me grasp the truth of the higher power concept. I'm no longer one of those who think there was some cosmic bang that sparked the world we live in, that we morphed from muddy ooze and over hundreds of thousands of years we ended up—us." He looked at her thoughtfully. "Sometimes if you want to know how to keep your engine running perfectly, you have to look to the manufacturer. You—and I—need to figure out who we were created to be—and be it. Once we have that down, then, and only then, can we open up and share ourselves with another human being without looking to them with unrealistic expectation."

She gazed back at him through tear-laced lashes, managed a smile. "You said you weren't poetic."

He laughed. "I'm not. The hard part is making the jump from here to there. Even that requires reliance on someone who is bigger than us."

"Now you're sounding like my dad."

Zane cocked his head. "Yeah? Is that a compliment?"

She nodded. "It is."

"Listen," he said. "I'm a straight shooter. I pretty much tell it like it is." He paused. "I'm extremely attracted to you. Might even say I hope to get to know you better, see where all this might lead. But be warned, I'm nobody's savior. I'm not here to fill you up."

Karyn absorbed his words like dusty land needing water. She reached and touched his cheek, ran her finger along the furrowed dimple at the side of his mouth.

With her heart pounding, she took a deep breath, walked to the garbage can in her kitchen and tossed the empty bottle inside.

She turned and looked at him. "You may not be a savior, but I think you may have just saved me."

23

L   eigh Ann pulled into Giacobbi Square, delighted to find
        a parking spot right in front of the Crane and Abbott
        law office. "Well, at least something is going right today,"
she told Karyn, who sat in her passenger seat. "You won't have to
walk far with that ankle."

Karyn undid her seat belt and grabbed her purse. "It's been
much better lately. I think I'm finally on the mend." Her face
broke into a little smile as she reached for the door handle.

Leigh Ann cut the engine. "Well, that's good news. I was
worried that injury was never going to heal." She exited the car,
stood in the late summer sunshine appreciating the flower boxes
filled with lantana, begonias and petite marguerite daisies. "If
only Joie could get this situation behind her as well."

Karyn shut her car door, joined her sister as she headed in the
direction of Joie's office. "I hate it too. Sometimes life can push
you in the gutter. In light of that, someone very wise reminded
me recently that if you want to keep your engine running
perfectly, you have to look to the manufacturer."

"Oh? How is Zane Keppner?"

Before Karyn could answer, the door to the Painted Lady Art

Studio swung open and Miss Trudy appeared, dressed in flowing zebra-print pants and a hot pink top. Her hair was wrapped up on her head in a matching scarf. "Well, hello girls! Heading to Joie's office? I think it's just awful that lawyer fellow from Boise is giving our sweet girl a hard time. Ruby and I have been worried sick about all the court shenanigans he's pulling."

"Hey, Miss Trudy," Karyn stopped, gave her a quick hug. "Please don't worry. I'm learning everything works out the way things are supposed to."

Leigh Ann took argument with that. "Oh, I don't know. From what Joie says, the courts are very reluctant to terminate a parent's rights."

Miss Trudy fingered a large gold earring dangling from her ear. "But the man signed some kind of document agreeing to give that sweet baby up," she reminded. "At least that's what Ruby and I heard. Doesn't that count for anything?"

Leigh Ann looked at their friend head on. "Andrew Merrill is a sly one, that's for sure. He petitioned to rescind and establish parental rights before the court finalized its order." She leaned in. "Apparently, he's using little Hudson to save his marriage."

A look of pure disgust sprouted on Miss Trudy's face. "That's despicable."

Karyn placed her hand on Leigh Ann's arm. "Perhaps we should get inside," she urged, then whispered as they moved on. "Not sure Joie would appreciate us sharing her private business."

"You mean *me*—and it's much better to get the right facts out there early. Public relations 101."

They walked the short distance to the law firm entrance. Inside, a woman with a gruff look on her face greeted them from behind a receptionist desk. From conversations with Joie, she knew her name. "Morning, Margaret."

"It's Margaret Adele," she corrected.

"What?"

"Margaret Adele—that's my name."

Leigh Ann's eyebrows lifted. "Oh, excuse me. Of course, Margaret Adele. Such a pretty name." She looked back at Karyn for support. Getting none, she continued, "Uh, we're here for a meeting with Maddy and our sister, Joie."

The woman hoisted her ample frame from her chair. "Follow me."

They walked through a beautifully decorated reception area, decorated a bit ornate for Leigh Ann's taste. The pale butter-yellow carpets were stunning, however. She had to remember to ask about them. They had to be custom dyed.

"Here you are." Margaret Adele opened a door to a conference room with windows overlooking Baldy and the vacant ski runs.

Maddy stood. "There you sweet things are!" She smoothed her floral printed taffeta skirt and moved to give them hugs. "I hope y'all adore chocolate tarts. I had Margaret Adele order us in some special." She leaned in. "They have just a touch of orange liqueur, but just a tad." She held up her forefinger and thumb and motioned, as if to make her point.

"Hi, you guys. Thanks for coming." Joie pointed them to a seat across from her. She looked wrecked.

"How are you holding up?" Karyn glanced between Joie and Clint, who sat perched near the end of the table looking a bit awkward. She nodded. "Hey, Clint."

Leigh Ann was surprised to see him there, and delighted. Her sister needed as many in her corner as she could get.

"I'm fine," Joie told them. "I just want to get all this behind me."

Maddy moved to the sideboard and filled her teacup. "Well, it's definitely in your benefit to put out the fire and call in the dogs. As I've explained, that is going to be easier said than done." She leaned against the sideboard and stirred her tea. Finished, she tapped the spoon on the rim of her dainty cup. "It should come as no surprise that Mr. Merrill has hired one of the best family law attorneys around—Jay Teeler." She looked at Joie. "You remember him from the custody matter we worked on a few months back."

Joie nodded, a sober look on her face. "He's good."

"Yes," Maddy agreed. "Another issue we will face is the low probability of prevailing on an out-and-out termination of rights. The fact of the matter is, Andrew Merrill is the father. If he wants to be part of Hudson's life, the court will likely support that."

Clint slammed his back against his chair in frustration. "That schmuck doesn't want to be a father. The way I see this whole thing is that he wants to avoid splitting his assets with a wife who is positioned to take him to the cleaners if she divorces him." He pointed to a stapled document on the table, his voice edged with desperation. "He's alleging Joie is a bad mother. What? Did he run out of puppies to kick?"

Leigh Ann shared his pain. None of this was fair. How fortunate she was to be married to Mark. Despite his business miscalculations, he was a good man, and a good father. She wanted that for her sister.

Now, more than ever.

~

JOIE STARED ACROSS THE TABLE. Maddy was talking, her voice sounding like it was coming through a tunnel.

"Let's talk a little bit about what to expect tomorrow," she said. "A stable environment is paramount to a child. Andrew's paternity is established—that's not the issue. Our fight will be to convince the court that shuffling little Hudson between Sun Valley and Boise will be detrimental to his well-being." She looked at Joie. "Joie, we've talked. You're aware that I intend to argue an infant should not be away from his mother for any length of time. We've stated that position in our initial response, and I can back that up with precedence, particularly a ruling in

Jones v. Jones that was affirmed by the appellate court." She paused, fingered the ruffles on her blouse. "Andrew and his counsel know this as well. We need to be ready for anything." She scooped and held up the document from the table. "They've already made clear that they intend to make an argument that little Hudson's current environment is already unstable—that Joie leads a reckless lifestyle and shuffles him between caretakers while she focuses on her career."

"But that's a lie!" Leigh Ann argued. "Joie has settled down. She's a wonderful mother. And we're all here helping her do that."

"It's not like he's with strangers," Karyn added. "For example, our father is sitting on his front porch right now rocking his grandson. Hudson is loved and well-cared for. How can they possibly argue differently?"

While Joie appreciated her sisters coming to her defense, she'd read the affidavit—the allegations that she had a history of drinking too much and living on the wild side. Sure, she'd changed—but there would be affidavits stating otherwise, photographs pulled from social media and blown up as exhibits in what she expected would be an ugly parade of her past life, highlighting every bad decision she'd ever made. A highly-paid team of investigators would dig up every potential piece of dirt.

Her heart thudded painfully. The only way for Andrew to win was to equalize the scales of justice—to paint her as an unstable person, thereby defusing the stability factor.

She swallowed against the tightness building in her throat. "I hear what you're telling me, Maddy. Andrew is coming after me —and he has nothing to lose."

Maddy grinned at that. "Oh, darlin'" she said, her eyes sparkling. "Mad Dog Maddy Crane is on your side. He has everything to lose."

24

The courthouse where the hearing would be held was in the county seat of Hailey, a town less than fifteen miles south of Sun Valley. While preferring to ride alone, Joie finally gave in and agreed to go in the car with Leigh Ann and Karyn. Hudson would remain behind with her father. "I'll support you any way you need me to, sweetheart," he'd told her. "Even if it means not being in that courtroom to hold your hand. Rest assured, I'll be praying. Besides," he added. "I'll take every chance I get to spend time with my little grandson. Yesterday, I had to fight Sebastian for the privilege of holding him during nap time."

"You don't have to hold him while he sleeps," Joie reminded him. "He does fine in his cradle."

"Nonsense. All you girls slumbered more soundly while in my arms."

Leigh Ann pulled into the already crowded parking lot. "Mark will be here later. He had an important meeting with—well, he'll be here in plenty of time for his turn on the stand."

Karyn pulled the visor down and checked her appearance in

the mirror. "I've never testified in court before. I'll admit to being a little nervous."

Joie peered out the windshield at the small crowd gathering on the courthouse steps, the realization of what was ahead like a millstone dragging her emotions under.

"It'll be fine," she told her sister, parroting what she'd told many clients. "Simply answer the questions the attorneys pose to the best of your ability. Don't feel pressured to answer before you're ready. More importantly, only answer what is asked. Nothing more." She stared a few seconds longer, scowled. "Is that a news truck?"

Leigh Ann nodded. "Looks like a station from Boise."

Karyn shut the visor and focused on the scene outside the car. "What in the world can they find newsworthy about a private custody matter?"

Leigh Ann cut the engine, slipped her hand over Joie's. "Everything's going to turn out fine. You'll see."

"What? Like the whole Preston U.S.A. thing? How did that turn out?" The minute the words slipped from her mouth, Joie knew she sounded mean. "I'm sorry, Leigh Ann. I'm—well, I—"

"You don't have to explain." Leigh Ann patted her arm. "Besides, the story is not over regarding Mark's business dealings."

Karyn reached for the door handle. "What do you mean, not over?"

Leigh Ann grabbed her purse and moved to get out of the car. "Just what I said."

The historic courthouse building was built in 1883 and was made of red brick with cast iron windowsills. Before they were halfway to the steps, a small group rushed to meet them, including Miss Trudy, Ruby and the guys that she used to hang out with at Crusty's. Nash Billingsley was there too, as was Father John.

"Oh, honey—we're here for you," Miss Trudy assured her, wrapping her arms around her waist and giving a hard squeeze.

Joie swallowed. "Thanks, everyone. I appreciate your support. I really do."

Inside, they made their way through security. Joie stood while a uniformed lady waved a wand down her torso.

Beyond, benches lined the hallway, mostly empty but for one where a teenage boy, sullen and angry looking, sat next to his mother. She wore slacks, shirt and a worn cardigan sweater. "See? I told you your choices would lead to no good."

A familiar ache sprouted. She leaned to her sisters. "Do I still have time to go to the restroom?"

Karyn checked her watch. "If you hurry."

The walls in the ladies' room were covered with tiny black and white tiles, the kind that were popular during the turn of the century. The basins were heavy porcelain with brass hardware. Frosted heavy glass windows, likely the originals, had been caulked tightly in place, leaving the air stifling and in dire need of air conditioning.

Some, including her sister Leigh Ann, would appreciate the vintage nature of the room. Joie only saw a worn-out décor that should have been replaced years ago.

Minutes later, after washing her hands, Joie turned off the water and grabbed for a paper towel. The mirror above the sink reflected a washed-out face mapped with worry. She ruffled through her bag to find the powder blush she'd slipped inside earlier. A heavy dose to the cheeks, and no one would suspect she was powering through this day on less than two hours sleep.

She heard a click, and the door to the stall farthest down the row swung open. At first, she failed to recognize the striking woman, but as the lady drew closer, Joie's breath caught.

Victoria Merrill—Andrew's wife.

She saw Joie about the same time. They both froze.

Joie tossed the compact back into her purse and flung it

over her shoulder, wanting desperately to ignore this unexpected encounter. "Ms. Merrill," she said in forced acknowledgement.

"That's *Mrs.* Merrill," the woman corrected—the same woman who was Hudson's step-mother, and depending on how this hearing went, the woman who might be tucking her son in bed at night. Joie couldn't afford to tangle with her. Especially not now, right before the hearing.

Collecting herself, she simply nodded. "Of course." She moved to slip around her, head for the door, but felt an arm on her own, stopping her.

"Just so you know, I forgive you." Victoria Merrill said the words with a smirk on her face.

For once, Joie knew better than to take the bait, stamped down her impulse to respond and tell her off. Instead, she simply nodded. "I need to go."

Victoria wouldn't release her hold. If anything, her red nails dug a little deeper. "That's what governor's wives do. We forgive and forget—at least for the benefit of the public."

There was something in the woman's eyes. A challenge that poked at Joie's sensibility. She couldn't resist pulling her arm free. "Governor?"

Andrew's wife laughed. "Oh? You haven't heard? An exploratory committee has asked Andy to consider running next year." Her eyes narrowed. "I can see the promo videos now, a little dark-haired toddler running into his daddy's arms, his adoring wife in the background."

Joie fought to breathe. This entire custody fight was a farce, a charade. The Merrills needed a stage prop and Hudson would fit the bill. Besides, how would it look if the perfect candidate abandoned his child?

Before she could respond, Victoria released her arm. "You may have weaseled into my husband's bed, but I'm the one he's leaving this hearing with—and soon, we'll be tucking your precious son into his car seat and taking him with us. So, I ask you—who's the winner here?"

That was more than Joie could take. She drew nose-to-nose. "Taking my son from me—*Mrs.* Merrill—will only happen over my dead body."

JOIE ENTERED THE HEARING ROOM, flanked by her sisters. She quickly glanced around the wood-paneled courtroom, took in the heavy draperies hanging at the windows, the marble columns on either side of the judge's bench up front. She drew a deep breath and made her way forward, leaving her sisters to sit in the gallery. She proceeded past the bar and sat at the counsel table next to Maddy, who reached and squeezed her hand. "You ready, sweet thing?"

Joie nodded, trying desperately to avoid looking across at Jay Teeler and his client. There was a time when she'd longed to be in the courtroom with Andrew, felt fortunate to be chosen to attend hearings at his side. Funny how abruptly everything could change.

She let her eyes drift past to where Victoria Merrill sat next to her husband, her meticulous face a pinched cathedral of propriety.

Joie couldn't help but consider all the hours she'd spent feeling guilty for hurting this woman. Yes, her affair had been wrong—but could it be Victoria Merrill was not so easily wounded?

Joie leaned to Maddy, lowered her voice to a terse whisper. "Before we begin, I need to tell you something." She quickly summarized what she'd learned from Andrew's wife.

Maddy winked, gave her a reassuring smile. "Trust me. I have everything under control."

A ripple of relief skated through her, again glad she had

Maddy by her side.

At the adjacent table, Jay Teeler unloaded a large black bag and placed a tall stack of files next to an expensive pen and yellow-lined tablet. Andrew's face broke into a smug grin as he lifted the water pitcher and filled his glass, then Victoria's.

Joie quickly diverted her gaze to the front, her anger almost palpable.

The bailiff stood. "All rise. Court is now in session, the Honorable Judge Rene Cole presiding."

The judge entered the courtroom, an older woman with white hair worn in a tightly-curled bob. She wore red-framed glasses and had a no-nonsense look about her. This person, who would decide their future, adjusted her robe and took her seat. "You may be seated."

The bailiff nodded, folded his hands in front of him. "Your Honor, today's case is a child custody matter entitled Merrill v. Abbott."

The clerk handed a file to the judge. "Thank you," she murmured, then directed her attention to the counsel tables. "I take it we're ready?"

Andrew's attorney stood, straightened his lapel. "May it please the court, my name is Jay Teeler, counsel for the petitioner in this action."

Maddy stood. "Madeline Crane, Your Hon-uh," she said in her southern drawl. "On behalf of the respondent."

"Thank you, both." Judge Cole scanned the contents of the file. "Okay, as I see it, paternity is not disputed. We have the father of the child wanting joint custody and making certain allegations, some of which imply that the current environment is unstable. The mother of the child is resisting on the basis of—" She looked over the top of her glasses at Maddy.

"On the basis Mr. Andrew Merrill and his so-called allegations are on a first name basis with the bottom of the deck."

Laughter broke out in the gallery, which prompted the judge to use her gavel.

"Apologies, Your Honor. What the petitioner and his counsel would like this court to believe is that my client, a dedicated mother who is a fellow member of the bar and my law partner, is unfit to be sole and full-time guardian of her son. That is hardly the truth, Judge Cole. The truth is Mr. Merrill initially relinquished his parental rights, only to change his mind to suit his political aspirations." Maddy waved her arm in the direction of the gallery. "We intend to refute these preposterous assertions and have numerous witnesses willing to testify as to Ms. Abbott's character and standing in her community."

"I see," the judge commented. "Mr. Teeler, do you have anything you want to add to your petition and affidavits before we begin?"

He shook his head. "No, Your Honor. Only to object to Ms. Crane's improper characterization of my client's desire to father his precious child. Beyond that, the filings we've lodged with the court stand on their own merit."

"So noted." the judge said. "Ms. Crane, how do you wish to proceed?"

"I'd like to call Leigh Ann Blackburn to the stand."

Her sister stood, gave Judge Cole a timid smile as she made her way to the witness stand and was sworn in. Every eye in the courtroom watched as the proceedings began.

"Please state your name for the record."

"Leigh Ann Blackburn."

Maddy smiled. "Thank yuh, Ms. Blackburn. And you are related to the respondent?"

Leigh Ann nodded. "Yes, I'm her older sister."

"Of three," Maddy said.

"Yes. I'm the oldest. Karyn is four years younger. Joie is the youngest."

Maddy's taffeta skirt made a swishing sound as she moved toward the witness box. "Tell us about your parents."

"Our mother died when I was fourteen. Daddy lives on a sheep ranch a few miles south of Sun Valley."

"That must've been hard on you girls, losing your mother at such an early age."

"Yes," Leigh Ann confirmed. "She was ill for many months. Nothing really prepares you for that kind of loss. You find a place to tuck the hurt inside your soul, but the pain follows you forever."

Maddy nodded with sympathy. "Tell us how that affected Joie."

Leigh Ann straightened, ready to recite the answer they'd practiced. "Joie was only five when Mom died. Of the three of us, she perhaps suffered the hardest blow. It's difficult at that age to understand the concept of death and the forever nature. She struggled to grasp that our mother was never coming home." Leigh Ann turned to the judge, made eye contact. "Despite that interruption, my little sister was smart and determined. She went to law school, clerked for a district judge for a short time, and then was thrilled to land a position as an associate in one of the most respected law firms in Boise."

"The law firm where the petitioner is a partner?"

Leigh Ann sighed. "Unfortunately, yes."

Maddy fingered the ruffle on her blouse. "Thank you. That is all."

Leigh Ann stood.

Mr. Teeler cleared his throat, held up an open palm. "Not too fast. I have a few follow-up questions."

Leigh Ann lifted her chin, sank back into her seat.

"Is it fair to say Joie had a wild side while growing up?"

"Excuse me? A wild side?"

He nodded. "Yes." He lifted a piece of paper from a file and walked toward the witness box. "I have a list of infractions she committed as a teenager—sneaking out, drinking with friends and running her father's stock truck into a telephone pole."

"Well, that was some time ago and—"

"And the stock truck was loaded with her friends, who had also been drinking?"

Leigh Ann's jaw stiffened. "I can assure you there is likely nothing on that list that I could not confirm. Joie found her way to being a sensible, and responsible adult after taking a path that wound around the mountain a bit." She squared her shoulders. "As you so eloquently noted, the stock truck was filled with other teenagers who didn't make the best decision that night. Joie's teenage antics are not that uncommon. I might add that one of those teens is now a law enforcement officer." Her sister looked directly at her. "Joie is an amazing woman who is talented and accomplished, a responsible woman who is a mother completely dedicated to her son."

Mr. Teeler returned to counsel table and retrieved another document, waved it in the air. "And yet, it was not that long ago you were called to Crusty's, a local liquor establishment, to retrieve your sister after receiving a call reporting she'd drunk multiple shots and was unable to drive herself home?"

Leigh Ann grew flustered. Despite Maddy's warnings that opposing counsel might try these antics, she didn't have a ready answer. "That's unfair. Joie—"

"Thank you," he said, cutting her off. "Now, turning to another matter—you have a history of overlooking family behavior that is lacking in good judgment, do you not? Isn't it true your own husband has been the subject of an FBI investigation into shady business practices?"

Leigh Ann nearly growled. "Hey, how did you—I mean, none of that is public knowledge. In fact, the truth is far from what you're intimating."

Maddy stood. "Objection, Your Honor." Without waiting for the judge to acknowledge her objection, she marched forward with her own document in hand. "May I clarify for the court, Your Honor?"

Mr. Teeler stepped back, swept his hand in a grand gesture. "By all means, Counselor. Clarify away." He returned to counsel table, patted his client's shoulder.

"Just a quick question, Ms. Blackburn. The matter introduced just now—the FBI investigation—your husband is working *with* the government investigators, isn't that right?"

Leigh Ann stubbornly lifted her chin. "Yes, that's correct."

"Mr. Blackburn is not the target of this investigation?"

"No, he's not."

"He's assisting the government in a matter having to do with his former business partner and her attempt to acquire Preston, USA?"

"That's absolutely correct."

An audible buzz broke out in the gallery. Miss Trudy gasped. She stood and hurried for the rear door, with her sister, Ruby, following close on her heels.

The news was obviously a surprise to everyone in the courtroom. Leigh Ann and Mark had held the information close to their chests, likely at the request of the investigators. Still, there was no doubt the news would spread soon, especially with the Dilworth sisters ready to do their part, and Mark would no longer be viewed as the villain in the story. At the very least, Joie was glad of that.

Maddy looked to the judge. "That's all I needed to clarify, Your Honor." She turned and looked to Mr. Teeler. "So the record is entirely accurate."

Judge Cole nodded. "Do you have anything further, Mr. Teeler?"

Andrew's attorney stood. "Yes, only a few more questions, Your Honor."

He approached the witness box. "Tell me about the day my client's son was born," he said, looking a bit like a panther on the prowl.

"What do you mean?" Leigh Ann asked, scowling.

Jay Teeler's face grew solemn. "I mean, explain to the judge the circumstances surrounding his birth that day—how your sister neglected to listen to reason and mounted a horse while in the end stages of her pregnancy, how she rode up a mountainside filled with rocky croppings and ended up delivering in the wilderness with no medical professionals to help her. Tell everyone here how, on day one, the mother of my client's son put her baby in danger."

Maddy interrupted with a steady voice. "Perhaps Mr. Teeler would like Ms. Blackburn to step down so he can take the stand and continue his testimony. He seems to know all about the facts in this matter."

The judge removed her glasses, tapped the on the table in front of her. "I believe the details of that day have all been included in your affidavit, Mr. Teeler, which I will take into due consideration. Unless this witness can provide further testimony, facts that I've not yet had an opportunity to review, then let's agree to move things along."

Mr. Teeler pursed his lips, nodded. "Yes, Your Honor. Just one follow-up question?"

"Granted."

Andrew's attorney looked at Leigh Ann. "Have you read my client's affidavit, the one we're discussing?"

She nodded.

The judge slipped her glasses back in place. "The recorder will need an audible answer."

"Oh, yes—sorry." Leigh Ann leaned into the microphone. "I have read the affidavit."

"Do you refute any of the facts stated therein?"

Her sister squared her shoulders, looked directly back at Mr. Teeler. "Only the part where you say my sister harmed little Hudson. He was fine then—and he's still fine. Joie is a good mother."

Mr. Teeler addressed the judge. "I guess that's a matter for this court to determine." Looking extremely satisfied, he returned to counsel table, leaned and whispered with his clients. When he'd finished, he stood. "That's all I have for this witness," he said, before returning to his seat.

Satisfied, Maddy glanced at Mr. Teeler. "That's all I have."

The judge clicked her pen closed and set it down. "Perhaps this is a good time to take a quick recess." She looked at the clock on the wall. "Let's reconvene in thirty minutes."

Joie felt Karyn's hand on her back, vaguely aware she was moving her out of the courtroom doors and into the hall. Leigh Ann, Father John and the others followed.

In the recesses of her mind, she heard Maddy remind everyone not to say a word until they got outside. Several feet ahead, Andrew hugged his wife.

Fighting to maintain control, Joie reminded herself to breathe as she brushed the wrinkles from her skirt with shaking fingers.

"Okay, that was what we call showboating. That's all Jay Teeler can do really, when his client is making an argument that is clearly an uphill battle." She grabbed Joie's hands. "The worst is over, darlin'. He's huffed and he's puffed, but he's failed to blow down anybody's house—especially yours."

Father John ran his arthritic fingers through what little hair he had left. "Let me up there. I can vouch for Joie."

Maddy's eyes twinkled. She placed a dainty hand on his forearm. "Thank you. But that won't be necessary. You'll see."

Joie excused herself, pulled her phone from her bag and called her father. "Hi, Dad. How's Hudson?"

"He's fine," he assured her. "Ate a good breakfast, and now he's sleeping soundly. Question is, how are you? How's the hearing going, sweetheart?"

"As well as can be expected," she admitted. "Maddy knows her stuff and she's not letting Andrew or his counsel make much headway. Still, this is grueling." She summarized the morning, avoiding describing how it had made her feel—that no matter how she'd tried to prepare herself, the terror of what was at stake nearly put her under.

"I've been praying for you all morning, Joie. We all have to keep reminding ourselves that God's in control. This will all work out, you'll see," he promised.

Joie pictured her dad on his knees and her frayed edges softened. "Thanks, Dad. That means more than I can express."

Her phone pinged.

"Sorry, Dad. I just got a message that it's time to go back in." She thanked him again and said goodbye, then scurried to make her way back through the security line.

Back inside the courtroom, court had already convened.

She quickly moved into her spot at counsel table. "Sorry I'm late," she whispered.

"No worries, darlin'. Everything okay with Hudson?"

Joie smiled, appreciating her law partner's unwavering intuition. "Yes. He's fine."

"Is counsel ready to begin?" the judge asked.

Maddy stood. "Yes, Your Honor." She fingered the hair at the back of her neck, smiled confidently. "I'd like to call Clint Ladner."

Joie's heart pounded as she watched her former boss make his way to the stand. After taking the oath, he sat, leaned back and folded his hands in his lap.

Despite the confident look on her law partner's face, Joie tensed. No one clued her in that Clint would be testifying. She detested surprises.

Maddy walked to the witness box. "Good morning, Mr. Ladner."

"Good morning," he said.

"I appreciate you being here today to support my client. I know it's not easy to take time off work."

He nodded. "No problem. Happy to do it."

Maddy smiled up at the judge. "Your Honor, you'll see Mr. Ladner was not on my original witness list, but it appears the truth put forth by the petitioner here today is about as scarce as hen's teeth."

Mr. Teeler spread his arms wide. "Your Honor, please—Ms. Crane here is mischaracterizing—"

Maddy laughed. "Oh, pooh! We both know you're hanging the wrong horse thief here."

A tiny smile nipped at corner of the judge's lips. No doubt, she'd read Joie's sworn affidavit as well. "Okay, let's stay focused, shall we?"

Maddy didn't miss a beat. "Of course, Your Honor." She returned her attention to the witness box. "Mr. Ladner, for the record, could you please state your full name?"

He leaned for the microphone. "Clinton Robert Ladner."

"Thank yuh, Mr. Ladner. And, you are close friends with my client, are you not?"

Clint grinned. "Yeah, Joie and I are close. Uh, friends," he quickly added.

Joie smiled at him, knowing he could testify for the next four hours and not fully disclose all the ways he'd been a friend to her. She remembered the day they met. She'd been over-confident, sassy—challenged him to a game of pool. Maybe he'd challenged her, she couldn't remember for sure. All she knew was she'd intended to win—and did. Turns out, in more ways than one.

She recalled the tender way he handled the wounded horse they'd rescued, the way he held her in the barn when she'd nearly fallen apart after realizing Andrew was a pathological liar. He'd given her emotional support without judgment when she found out she was pregnant, even drove her to Boise to confront Andrew. Right now, her little boy slept in a bed Clint made especially for him. There was no arguing Clint Ladner had been there for her, on the mountain when Hudson was born—and even now.

What would prompt a man who was that good looking, that sure of himself, to remain by her side when any number of women would fall at his cowboy boots, if given the opportunity? Especially given all her baggage.

The answer slowly dawned. She felt tears filling her eyes but was powerless to stop them.

"And you were her former boss, isn't that correct?"

"Yes," he told her. "She worked with me at the Sun Valley Stables. Joie Abbott was one of my best horse trainers. She also covered when needed and guided horseback tours."

"I see."

Joie blinked hard, fought to gain control of her emotions. This was no time to lose it.

Maddy fingered the pearls at her neck, gave Clint an encouraging smile. "Perhaps the court would benefit from hearing a little more about Joie and her relationship with her son, from an outsider's perspective."

"Sure." He adjusted his frame in the chair, trying to get comfortable.

Their eyes met.

"I think—" he said, choosing his words carefully. "Well, when I first met Joie, she was like a meteor jetting through the Milky Way. She had a way of shining brightly and moving at streak-speed—so fast, I could barely keep up. I mean, she's a force, you know?"

Joie felt her body flush, her spirit flip.

"Then little Hudson appeared on the scene." He smiled. "Don't get me wrong. She's still lives like a shooting star, but now that little boy is the sun. Her entire world revolves solely around him." He swallowed, looked directly at her. "Watching her face when she gazes at him—well, it's like she's now dancing on rays of light."

He rubbed his palms across the top of his jeans, his cheeks flushed. "Sorry, I didn't mean to—I guess what I'm trying to say— Joie Abbott cherishes her little boy. She's a great mother. That's all I really have to say."

Everyone remained quiet for a moment. Even Victoria seemed mesmerized as the judge straightened in her seat, adjusted her robe. "Thank you, Mr. Ladner." She drilled an unwavering look at counsel table. "Mr. Teeler? Any cross?"

There was a long pause. Mr. Teeler coughed. "No—I have no questions."

"In that case, let's move on."

The skin on Joie's shoulder's prickled as she watched Clint leave the stand and make his way back to the gallery. As he walked past counsel table, she gave him a grateful smile.

His dimple appeared as he smiled back at her.

25

"Respondents call the petitioner, Mr. Andrew Merrill, to the stand."

Jay Teeler bolted from his chair. "Objection! This is a custody hearing, not a trial. It's highly prejudicial to expect my client to provide testimony intended to assist the respondent in this matter."

Judge Cole frowned, looked down at counsel table. "In case you haven't noticed, there is no jury to prejudice. I'm certain you are not implying that I am unable to sort through the testimony provided and come to a reasonable and legally-backed decision —are you?"

Mr. Teeler slumped back down. "No, Your Honor. Certainly, that was not my intent. I simply meant to—"

The judge banged her gavel. "Overruled." She looked to Maddy. "You may proceed."

Andrew patted his wife's hand, whispered something in her ear before standing. He straightened his tie, then marched to the witness box.

The bailiff stepped forward. "Please raise your right hand."

Andrew complied. He coughed.

"Do you swear the testimony you are about to provide is the truth, the whole truth, and nothing but the truth, so help you, God?"

Andrew nodded. "I do."

The heels on Maddy's shoes clicked against the polished floor tiles as she marched forward. "Mr. Merrill, could you please state your name for the record."

He leaned toward the microphone. "Andrew Merrill."

"No middle name?"

"No," he responded. His lips returned to a tight line.

"And, you are married to Victoria Merrill?" Maddy turned and pointed. "The woman sitting with you at counsel table?"

Andrew made a point of rolling his eyes. "Yes, my wife is sitting with me at counsel table."

"Thank, yuh." She turned, nodded to Quinn Ferrari, the firm's legal investigator, who sat near the rear courtroom door.

Heads turned and everyone followed as Quinn stood and opened the door. In walked a stunning woman who looked to be in her mid-twenties. She had long blonde hair that cascaded over her shoulders in careless curls. She wore a simple, black wrap skirt with a top in a pretty shade of pink.

Joie gave Maddy a puzzled look. Her attorney simply smiled and returned her focus to the witness box.

Andrew adjusted his collar.

"Now, Mr. Merrill—could you tell Judge Cole when you first met Joie Abbott."

He swallowed, continued to look at the young woman who had entered the courtroom and now sat by Quinn. "We met in— uh, I think it was three years ago. As testified to earlier, she was an associate with my law firm in Boise."

"Thank yuh, sir. Now, at what point did you start sleeping with my client?"

Andrew's eyes narrowed. Clearly Maddy's question had him on the defensive. "I—uh," he looked at Victoria. "I don't recall an exact date, but I'd guess she'd been employed about six months."

"I see." Maddy turned and nodded at Quinn a second time.

Quinn stood and opened the door. A second woman entered the courtroom, this time a coltish-looking brunette, with a short haircut lifted into chunky spikes. Joie immediately recognized her as the clerk from the Grove Hotel, where she and Andrew often used to slip off to in the afternoons.

Behind her walked another girl with gorgeous hair the color of butterscotch. She wore a cream-colored suit and heels, carried a Kate Spade briefcase.

From the front of the courtroom, Maddy cleared her throat. "Mr. Merrill?"

Andrew returned his attention to Joie's law partner, his face flushed. "Yes?"

Maddy smiled. "Do you need a drink of water?"

He coughed. "No. No, I'm fine."

She nodded. "Good. Now, I think we can dispense with the details of the way you cheated on your wife and had an affair with my client. Let's jump to when you found out Joie was pregnant." Maddy strolled slowly back to where Joie sat, retrieved the document he'd signed that day Clint took her to Boise.

The memory and the building drama in the courtroom caused a tiny trickle of sweat to run down Joie's back. If the stakes weren't so incredibly high, she'd bolt. Only Hudson was worth this.

Maddy handed the document to Andrew. "This is your signature?"

Andrew continued to stare at the women sitting in the gallery. "Yes," he admitted, his voice barely audible.

The courtroom door opened again. This time Wendy Riggs entered, the paralegal who was at Andrew's house the day Joie told him she was pregnant and he'd signed the relinquishment papers. She took a seat next to the others.

From the tiny window in the door, Joie could see there were more waiting their turn.

It suddenly dawned on Joie what Maddy was up to. She looked across at Andrew's wife. Victoria's hands were shaking as she clasped the table, stood. She grabbed her bag and despite the attorney's attempts to stop her, she marched past the bar, down the aisle and out the door.

In the witness box, Andrew shut his eyes, clamping them tight. When he opened them, he looked at Jay Teeler, who seemed positively perplexed.

"That's enough," Andrew said.

Mr. Teeler raised his eyebrows. "I'm sorry, but—"

"I said that's enough," Andrew barked. "It's over. I withdraw my petition." He clamored out of the witness box and followed after Victoria.

Applause broke out in the galley.

The judge banged her gavel. "That's enough. Settle down."

Maddy's face broke into a wide grin as she turned to face the judge. "Well, Your Honor—I guess that's all my questions. Respondent rests."

Judge Cole rose from her seat. "I'd like to see counsel in my chambers!"

Joie smiled, glanced back at her sisters, then at Clint. His eyes were filled with emotion. He touched two of his fingers to his lips and motioned as if blowing a kiss—a gesture that made her heart speed up. At that moment, it sank in what he'd said on the stand was spot on.

Despite all the changes of the past year, all her past poor choices, today she was different. Even more, with the threat of losing Hudson gone, she truly was free to dance across the Milky Way.

26

The morning following the custody hearing dawned bright and crisp, promising the kind of sunlit day Sun Valley was known for. The lane leading to the Abbott Ranch was lined with trees showing early signs of autumn, signaling a shift of season was on its way. Tufts of grass at the base of the fence posts now showed touches of color, tones that matched the spices in Leigh Ann's kitchen cupboard—cumin, sage and cloves. Change was definitely in the air.

Leigh Ann leaned her head against the back of the rocking chair on her father's porch. "Happy looks good on you, Joie."

"Yeah? Well, everything looks good on me," she quipped.

Leigh Ann rolled her eyes. "Especially that necklace of humility hanging around your neck."

Joie patted Hudson's bottom as she rocked her sleeping son in the neighboring chair. "I got it on Amazon." Her expression softened. "But thanks, I am happy."

Leigh Ann took a drink from her glass of iced tea. "Seriously, Joie. I'm proud of the way you handled this whole Andrew thing. For once, you stepped back and didn't try to win the fight all on your own.

Joie scowled. "Gee—was that supposed to be a compliment?"

Leigh Ann waved her off. "Don't you remember in the third grade when Vince Cartwright called you a doody head?"

"What has that got to do with anything?"

"Everything. As I remember, you wrestled him to the ground and beat the lemons out of him. Dad had to go the school and—"

"Oh, yeah—that. Well, believe me—if Maddy hadn't pulled her magic in that courtroom, I'd have had no problem pounding on Andrew in whatever way available. He and that ambitious wife of his were never getting their hands on Hudson, not while I was still breathing." She felt a lump rising in her throat. "When he's old enough, he can choose whether or not to have a relationship with that man. He—well, he wasn't who I thought he was. Turns out tequila is the liquid version of Photoshop. Enough shots, and you see only what you want to see."

Leigh Ann lifted the rolled newspaper from her lap. "Well, looks like a lot of potential constituents will sober up after reading the news this morning. It's not likely Andrew and Victoria will be moving into the governor's mansion anytime soon—not after that parade of women showed up. Can anyone say hashtag *Me Too*?"

Joie kissed the top of Hudson's downy head. "Yeah, doesn't take much to ruin a reputation."

Her sister nodded. "I've been on the pointed end of that stick. This whole town, including me, had Mark skewered and were ready to roast him. We didn't see that, despite his mistakes—in the end, he was only trying to make things right." She paused, took a deep breath. "The truth is, all of us have the potential to veer off course. The true measure of a person is whether we are willing to change."

"So, what's going to happen to that investment lady?"

"Mark's former partner?"

Joie nodded. "Yeah, sounds like she was something."

Leigh Ann's expression grew thoughtful. "Greed can do awful

things to people. Mark really learned a lesson. Not everyone can be trusted."

Joie shifted Hudson onto her arm, tucked the light blanket under his chin. "You got that right. Still, just because you do a terrible thing, it doesn't mean you are a terrible person. I, of anyone, know that. Maybe Mark's partner originally meant well, and just went terribly off course."

Leigh Ann stared at the sky. "Well, the FBI will finish their investigation and it will all end the way it's supposed to. Mark thinks there will be a plea deal. And by helping the prosecutors, Mark revived his own reputation to some extent."

A loud rumbling in the distance caught their attention. A motorcycle barreled down the lane, a plume of dust trailing behind.

Leigh Ann stopped rocking, leaned forward. "Is that a motorcycle?"

Joie shrugged. "Not sure, but I think it's safe to rule out that it's a horse. Sounds like a Harley."

"How can you know that?"

Joie stood, watched the bike maneuver the final bend in the lane. "The crankshaft in a Harley engine has only one pin, and both pistons connect to it. This design, combined with the V arrangement of the cylinders—" She scowled. "Whoever it is had better slow down before they lay that thing over on its side."

Leigh Ann glanced over at her younger sister with a smile. "Interesting advice—especially coming from someone who's kicked up more dust on that road than anyone I know."

The motorcycle roared into the yard and the rider cut the engine, slipped the kickstand into place. Off came the helmet.

Joie stopped patting Hudson's bottom. "Karyn?"

Leigh Ann bolted up. "What in the world?" She exchanged puzzled glances with Joie.

Karyn removed her Roka sports glasses from her face, untethered her long brown hair and let it cascade down her back. "Hey, sorry I'm late. What'd I miss?"

Leigh Ann clambered down the porch steps, nearly tripping over her father's dog's tail. "Move, Riley girl, before I step on you," she said, as she made her way to Karyn.

Joie snapped her fingers. "C'mon, Riley. You'd best stay over here. Hurricane Leigh Ann is blowing through."

Her oldest sister swiveled and gave her a pointed look.

Joie grinned at her. "Oh, c'mon. Lighten up."

Ignoring her, Leigh Ann made her way to Karyn, curiously examined the bike. "What in the world? I mean, what are you —seventeen?"

Karyn's eyes sparkled with laughter. "Well, I'm no longer going to act like I'm sixty-five—metaphorically speaking."

With Leigh Ann following close behind, Karyn climbed the porch steps. "Hey, Joie!"

"Hey, to you too." Joie exchanged another confused look with Leigh Ann before focusing back on her middle sister. "You okay?" Joie ventured.

"I'm fine. Why shouldn't I be?" Karyn's boots scuffed against the wood on the porch as she made her way to the third rocking chair and sat.

Joie wasn't one to dance around the bush. "What's with you and the bike?"

Karyn shrugged and picked something off her jeans. "Oh, that."

"Yes, that," Leigh Ann said, bending to pat Riley on the head. "Who does it belong to?"

Karyn grinned. "Me!"

"You bought a motorcycle?" Leigh Ann asked, her eyes wide.

Karyn leaned back against her rocking chair, unable to contain her smile. "Not just any motorcycle. It's a Harley-Davidson Softail Deluxe, part of their twin engine line-up." She leaned forward and said to Joie, "Sixteen ninety cc's of pure horsepower and torque."

Joie raised her brows, nodded her head. "Impressive."

Leigh Ann couldn't take it any longer, she held up both palms. "Wait—you bought a motorcycle?"

"Um-hmm."

"Goodness sakes, why would you do that?" Leigh Ann shook her head. "I have enough to worry about—a son stationed on the front lines in some war zone thousands of miles away, with no way of reaching him. Days and nights of worry, waiting to get some awful text telling me he's been injured—or worse, killed. I've been sick thinking about Joie's hearing and Mark's failed business, and now I have to worry about you splattering yourself on some highway?" She threw her hands up in the air. "Can't anybody give me a break, here?"

Before anyone could respond, Leigh Ann parked her hands on her hips. "What in the world prompted you go all biker-girl?" She shook her head, turned to Joie. "This just isn't Karyn."

Joie couldn't help but laugh. "Looks like you've got some 'splaining to do, Lucy."

Karyn fixed her eyes on her sisters. "I'm going on a trip," she announced.

"A trip? Where? When?" Leigh Ann's questions came like rapid-fire artillery. An idea formed. "Does this have anything to do with that food photographer—Zane what's-his-name?"

"Zane Keppner." A self-satisfied smile broke out across Karyn's face. "And yes, he's invited me to go on a cross-country ride, well not exactly the entire country. Zane is going to take some time off and we're going to head north, explore Glacier National Park, then make our way through Yellowstone and head for northern California. He'll be on assignment for *Food Critic Magazine* and is going to shoot the opening of a new winery and restaurant in Sonoma." She started rocking. "And before either of you jump to conclusions, we're just friends. He taught me an important lesson."

"Which is?" Leigh Ann asked.

"When you get shoved out of the tree and you're in free fall, you can't wait for someone to fly underneath and save you. You have to save yourself."

The baby started fussing. Joie stood and lifted him back to her shoulder. "Wow, so you are heading out on the big adventure. I mean, that's great and everything, but what about your job?"

"I talked to Jon last night. He's more than willing to allow Leigh Ann to cover for me while I take a leave of absence."

Leigh Ann's eyes widened. She didn't know what she'd expected, but not this. "But what about Vanguard?"

Karyn smiled, rubbed her fingers against the worn wooden armrests. "All the important decisions have been made and everything is in place. You already met with Horace Mikel and he's completely comfortable with your ideas and direction. The transition will be seamless." Her gaze grew steady. "We both know you are perfect for the job." She let out a light laugh. "But, don't get too comfortable. I'm coming back."

"Yes, well—" She'd been about to make a remark about being happy to fill in, provided the situation was indeed temporary, when she spotted Clint Ladner's truck coming down the lane. "Looks like you have company, Joie." Her eyes sparkled with amusement. "Or, should I just refer to him as your *friend*."

Karyn withdrew a band from her jeans pocket, pulled her hair back and fastened it into a ponytail. "Yeah, we both saw the way Clint looked at you when he was up on that stand—what he said. That guy's definitely into you."

Leigh Ann nodded smugly. "Yup—he's smitten. Just as I predicted."

Joie gave a strange, unreadable look. "Look, both of you—you've got it all wrong."

JOIE TOOK A DEEP BREATH IN—THEN let it out.

In—out.

There weren't enough calming breaths in the world to settle Joie's sudden attack of nerves as she watched Clint's truck come to a stop in the yard, heard him cut the engine.

Truth was, she knew her sisters weren't all that far off in their assessment regarding the way Clint felt about her. She, too, had seen something in his eyes yesterday—a tenderness that made her ache. A good kind of ache that spread all through her, making her legs go weak.

She leaned her cheek against Hudson's tiny head, smiled. If she were honest, she suspected he'd felt that way about her for some time.

She watched Clint climb from his truck, run his hand through his thick, brown hair. Their eyes locked and he waved.

Her heart raced. She was scared to death to want Clint—or believe that he wanted her. She simply couldn't afford to make any more mistakes. Up to now, she hadn't exactly made a good run of it. She'd made a practice of moving on impulse, letting her wants and desires direct her decisions.

Hudson deserved better than that.

Leigh Ann grinned, extended her arms. "Here, give me that baby." She gently lifted Hudson from Joie's arms and motioned for Karyn to follow her inside, leaving Joie standing alone on the porch as Clint approached.

"Hey," he said, bending to pat Riley's back.

"Morning," she said.

"Where'd your sisters take off to?"

She chuckled. "I'm sure they're standing just inside with their ears pressed against the crack in the door. Isn't that right, Leigh Ann?" she called over her shoulder.

The door suddenly shut tight. Joie rolled her eyes. "I told you."

Clint laughed out loud. "Let's go for a walk," he suggested, taking her hand.

The adrenaline coursing through Joie's veins drained suddenly, leaving her weak and shaky. She'd never considered herself the kind of woman who yearned for a knight in shining armor, but just the feel of his calloused palms against her own made the notion appealing.

"So, I know I told you how grateful I was for your testimony yesterday," she said. "But, I just wanted to thank you again. It meant everything. Not only to the court process, but to me."

She could feel him watching her as they passed the barn and headed for the creek.

"I mean, no one has ever said such nice things about me," she told him. "Well, except my sisters. They're family. They're supposed to say nice things."

Clint pocketed his hands, walked alongside her. "That Maddy is something. No doubt, she's the one who saved the day. I'm so glad everything ended the way it did, Joie. For your sake, and for Hudson's." A frown crossed his face. "I knew that guy, Andrew, was a creep the moment I met him."

"Yeah—he was not one of my shining moments," Joie admitted. "Thankfully, he's agreed to fully relinquish all parental rights and won't be a part of Hudson's life going forward. I mean, never one time did he ask to see him. That tells you something."

They came to a stop next to the creek. For several moments, they simply stood and listened as water trickled over the stone riverbed. Suddenly, Clint was so close she could smell the mixture of wood and lemon scents in his cologne. The aroma tightened her gut, pushed a smile onto her lips.

She'd never allowed herself to think too much about it before, but have mercy, he was hot. Memories of the day she first met him played across the screen of her mind—the way he wore those jeans the bar. How he'd flirted, and she'd flirted right back.

Who knew where everything might have led had she not discovered Clint was her new boss, or had Andrew not shown back up on the scene?

She'd foolishly believed life was like jumping from a plane— you could simply freefall until you landed someplace safe. Unfortunately, she'd discovered you could land in the briars and thistles. Sure, she could maneuver life without a mate, but she now realized she didn't want to.

In her clumsy way, she'd almost admitted that to Clint that night before the hearing.

"Joie?"

She saw the corner of Clint's lip tilt up ever so slightly, his eyes soften. Instinctively, she relaxed, knowing she was safe with him. He would never hurt her.

"Yeah?"

Clint stared at her with big, hopeful eyes. "We need to talk."

Feeling uncharacteristically self-conscious, she glanced down to discover her shirt wasn't buttoned right after nursing. Her nerves got the best of her—she giggled as her fingers quickly moved to remedy the problem.

His hand cupped her own.

Their eyes met and she couldn't look away. Her heart sped up as he cleared his throat. "Joie," he said, somehow infusing her name with desire. "Joie, if you love someone, you tell 'em, even if you're scared for more reasons than you can count, even if you're scared that it'll cause problems, even if you're scared that it'll burn your life to the ground. You say it. Out loud."

Clint paused, took a deep breath. "I love you, Joie. I love you in a really, really big—pretend I like your music, let you have the last piece of cheesecake, sing off key outside your window—love you." He squeezed her fingers. "I love you and I'm always going to love you." He paused. "But, I don't only want to love you. I want to make you happy."

Her lashes spiked with moisture. With her free hand, she reached and traced his jawline, felt the coarseness of his stubble against her skin.

He closed the space between them and kissed her slowly. His stomach was hard against hers, his shoulders like solid rock.

He deepened the kiss and she responded in kind, drawing her fingers through his hair.

She latched onto the thought that this is what she'd always longed for. With the thought came complete surrender. She ran her hands along the plane of his back and returned the kiss with fervor.

He pulled back, putting space she didn't want between them. "Joie," he said, his breath ragged. His eyes were deep shadows of longing, mirroring her own. "Marry me," he whispered. "Let me take care of you, and Hudson."

He looked at her the way every woman yearned to be looked at. Like she was cherished. She dared to return the gaze, never having known love could feel like this.

"Are—are you sure?" she asked. "I mean, like you said on the stand yesterday, I can be a handful."

Clint threw his head back, laughed out loud. "Yes, no one knows that more than me." He clasped her face in his hands. "Here's the good part, so listen close. I want you to grow old with me, Joie Abbott. You're the one I want to wake up with and go to bed with and do everything in between with. Marry me."

She lifted his fingers to her lips, kissed his knuckles. "Yes," she said, tears now rolling down her cheeks. She laughed. "Okay, yes. I'll marry you."

27

Karyn pulled back the curtain, peeked out the window. "Leigh Ann—come look!" She glanced back at her sister with excitement. "Joie and Clint are down at the creek and he's kissing her!"

"Get out! Let me see." Leigh Ann rushed to the window. She wedged herself where she could get a good look. Her face immediately broke into a bright smile. "Ha—I knew it was only a matter of time." She gazed at her baby nephew. "Hudson, you're far too young to understand the world of love, but things are definitely looking up out there."

The baby cooed, waved his pudgy arms.

Leigh Ann laughed as she handed him off to Karyn and headed for the kitchen. "I guess this means Joie won't be helping us with these tomatoes." She unpacked mason jars from a box at her feet and set them on the counter.

Karyn grinned down at her little nephew. "Would you remind your Aunt Leigh Ann we all still have cupboards full of tomatoes from last summer?"

Her older sister waved her off. "Oh, stop. You can never have too many tomatoes."

Karyn peeked out the window again. "Hey, Dad's home." She frowned, leaned on her tippy toes for a better look. "I think he's got somebody with him. Two somebodies—" She paused mid-sentence, not believing what she was seeing. Her face broke into a wide smile. "Leigh Ann, you'd better come take a look."

"I will, after I finish getting out these jars."

Karyn raced for the kitchen. "I think you'd better come now." She grabbed her sister's arm and pulled her toward the front door, flung it open. "Look!"

Leigh Ann's hand went to her mouth as she audibly gasped. "Colby?" She nearly screamed as she said it. "Colby!"

She ran across the porch, scrambled down the stairs with arms out and tears streaming down her face. Their dad's pickup barely came to a stop before she flung the passenger door open, pulled her son from the seat and pulled him into a tight embrace. "Why didn't you tell me?"

Colby laughed. "I wanted to surprise you." He picked his mother up and swung her around. "Did you miss me?"

Riley circled their feet and barked, his tail wagging.

"Miss you? Oh—you have no idea." Leigh Ann pointed her finger at her daughter-in-law who had now exited the truck as well. "You! How did you keep this a secret, Nicole?"

She shrugged. "It wasn't easy, I'll give you that."

Their father looked around. "Where's Joie?"

Karyn pointed in the direction of the creek. Clint and Joie were walking toward them, hand-in-hand.

Their dad grinned at the sight. "Well, it's about time."

Leigh Ann grasped her son's face between her hands. "Let me look at you. Are you okay? Looks like you lost some weight. Did they feed you okay?"

He assured his mother he had eaten just fine while away.

Leigh Ann pulled her phone from her pocket. "I have to text your father—tell him the news."

Joie waved as she neared. "Hey, everybody! What is all the—"

She stopped talked mid-sentence and stared in unbelief. "Colby? Is that you?" She broke from Clint and ran forward, hugged her nephew. "Welcome home, buddy!"

Clint reached and shook Colby's hand. "Yeah, welcome back."

Leigh Ann swiped away her tears. "Well, come inside everyone. I'll fix lunch."

Joie exchanged glances with Clint. "First, I've got news."

Everyone stopped, directed their attention her way. "What news?" Leigh Ann demanded. "I'm not sure my heart can take any more surprises."

Karyn's face drew into a knowing smile. "Leigh Ann—she has news."

Leigh Ann raised her eyebrows. "Oh, my goodness—you have *news*?"

Joie laughed, folded her hand inside Clint's. "Yes, we have news." She grinned and lifted her left hand, showing off a diamond engagement ring. "It's official—Clint and I are getting married."

"Oh my goodness! That's wonderful. When?" Leigh Ann folded her sister in her arms, her eyes filled with excitement. "We'll have a lot to do. Book the church, flowers, assemble a guest list." She turned and embraced Clint. "Congratulations."

Joie held up her hands. "There's plenty of time for all that. We intend to wait until Karyn gets back from her adventure. So, we're thinking maybe after the first of the year sometime."

Karyn gazed at her younger sister, smiled. "That sounds lovely."

Amidst a flurry of congratulations that followed, Joie lifted her son from Karyn's arms, her face revealing deep happiness.

Karyn drew a deep breath, pondering how so much had changed.

Resenting Grayson for leaving her was far too exhausting. She didn't want to do it anymore. Hanging on was too painful. She had no choice but to embrace change, let go.

Besides, perhaps change happened for a reason. She was getting a chance to begin again—a new beginning that meant trading in loss for a grand adventure—on a Harley, no less. Something she would never have considered a year ago.

With Colby home, Leigh Ann could quit worrying—at least for now. Andrew was no longer a threat. Joie could shed her shame and was finally free to fully embrace happiness—with Clint.

Karyn placed her arm around Leigh Ann, embraced Joie with her other arm. She gave them both a squeeze as they crossed the porch and headed inside. "C'mon, girls. We have tomatoes waiting."

Despite all the changes they'd endured, her sisters were happy. She was happy.

Change—most people didn't like it, at times even feared it—but no one could stop it from coming. The truth was, sometimes —oh, sometimes change was good. Sometimes, change was everything. And sometimes, against all odds, against all logic, change provided new reasons to look at the future with hearts brimming with hope.

AFTERWORD

Hey, everybody—Miss Trudy here. Kellie and I are so glad you joined us for another story in the Sun Valley Series. Don't you just love how each of these sisters faced major change—and adapted?

And, girls! Clint and Joie are getting married!

I just love weddings, and I hope you'll join us for the next instalment of the Sun Valley series—*PROMISES* (releases Summer, 2019)

Anyway, sweet things, Kellie is writing as fast as she can. Make sure and sign up for her **newsletter** so you get notices when future books in the series are available. Don't forget to check out all the information on Sun Valley she has on her **website** at www.kelliecoatesgilbert.com (PS—that's her home-town area!)

You might also enjoy Kellie's new **LOVE ON VACATION** stories. These shorter length romances invite readers to come on vacation with characters who travel to Sun Valley and stay at the iconic Sun Valley Lodge. This groundbreaking series is packed with tales of dating and mating, love and marriage and promises to keep your emotions and your funny bone on high alert. You'll also see a few recognized characters from the Sun Valley series books show up on occasion. Check out the first story, **Otherwise Engaged**.

Well, I've got to scoot. I have to shop for a dress to wear to that wedding. But, we'll see each other again soon!

~Miss Trudy

*Disclaimer – The Sun Valley Series and the Love on Vacation books are not associated with the City of Sun Valley, Sun Valley Resort, Sun Valley Company or Sinclair Oil Co. These books are solely the creative works of Kellie Coates Gilbert and Amnos Media Group.

ABOUT THE AUTHOR

Kellie Coates Gilbert has won readers' hearts with her compelling and highly emotional stories about women and the relationships that define their lives. A former legal investigator, she is especially known for keeping readers turning pages and creating nuanced characters who seem real.

In addition to garnering hundreds of five-star reviews, Kellie has been described by RT Book Reviews as a "deft, crisp storyteller." Her books were featured as Barnes & Noble Top Shelf Picks and were included on Library Journal's Best Book List of 2014.

Born and raised near Sun Valley, Idaho, Kellie now lives with her husband of over thirty-five years in Dallas, where she spends most days drinking sweet tea by a pool and writing the stories of her heart.

Please visit her at:

WWW.KELLIECOATESGILBERT.COM

Don't miss out on new releases and special contest information!
If you haven't signed up for **Kellie's newsletter** ... what are you
waiting for? **Click here!**

ALSO BY KELLIE COATES GILBERT:

Sisters (Sun Valley Series Book 1)

Heartbeats (Sun Valley Series Book 2)

Changes (Sun Valley Series Book 3)

Promises (Sun Valley Series Book 4)

Otherwise Engaged – a Love on Vacation Story

All Fore Love – A Love on Vacation Story

A Woman of Fortune – Texas Gold Book 1

Where Rivers Part – Texas Gold Book 2

A Reason to Stay – Texas Gold Book 3

What Matters Most – Texas Gold Book 4

Mother of Pearl

More information and purchase links can be found at:

www.kelliecoatesgilbert.com

SNEAK PEEK - A WOMAN OF FORTUNE

Until today, Claire Massey had never been inside the walls of a federal prison.

She'd taken French cooking lessons in Paris, photographed the aurora borealis, and even dined with a president and his wife. But never in her wildest imagination could she have contemplated herself doing this.

She fingered the fine-grain leather bag in her lap as the car slowly moved through heavy metal gates and past the guard tower that strangely resembled a childhood fort.

"You okay, Mom?"

She startled at her son's voice. "What? Uh, yes, I'm fine." Her hand plunged inside her purse for her Dolce & Gabbana sunglasses.

Max took a deep breath. "You don't have to do this, you know."

Claire nodded, keeping her eyes averted from the razor wire that cut a line across the horizon. She slipped the glasses on, glad for the barrier between her budding tears and the harsh Texas sun reflecting off the building looming ahead.

She swallowed. Hard. This was no time to lose it.

After pulling one hand from the steering wheel, her son slipped his palm over her trembling fingers. "Please, Mom, let me go in with you."

She shook her head. "No, this is something I need to do. Alone."

Max circled the parking lot twice before finding an empty spot. He pulled the car between a pickup with wheels the size of her car door and a battered green sedan that had definitely seen better days. From its rearview mirror hung a rosary and a pair of red lace panties, the kind you might see on a Victoria's Secret model.

Her son cut the engine.

Claire took a deep breath. "I don't know how long this will take."

Something in Max's eyes dimmed. He scratched at his beard stubble. "I'll be here."

The line at the front door extended several hundred yards. Claire moved with caution into place at the end, behind a heavy woman clothed in a stained housedress and slipper-like shoes that dug deeply into swollen flesh.

She shifted uncomfortably in her own wedge pumps, aware she'd made a questionable shoe choice. Why hadn't she thought to wear tennis shoes? The woman she'd talked to on the telephone yesterday warned Saturday was their heaviest day for visitors, cautioning the line would be like this.

Forty minutes passed before Claire reached the front-entry door and stepped into the large, old brick building and out of the baking sun, the inside air a welcome respite from the heat emanating from the concrete she'd been standing on. Despite the cooler temperature, sweat formed on her scalp. The heat perhaps? Or maybe nerves. She couldn't tell.

From somewhere in the line behind her, a young girl shushed her squalling infant. Claire couldn't help but think this was no place for a baby. But then again, would any of them be here if given a better option?

A woman officer dressed in a blue shirt, damp at the underarms, stepped forward. "I'll need your driver's license." She thrust a clipboard at Claire. "Sign at the designated spot and put the time next to your name." She tilted her head toward a large clock on the opposite wall. "And place your belongings in the basket."

Claire looked up. "My belongings?"

The woman sighed. "Rings, watch. You can't take nothing in with you."

"But my purse—"

"Nothing," she repeated.

Claire swallowed and did as she was told. When finished, she held up the basket to the officer.

The woman pointed to a wall lined with lockers and handed Claire a key. "Over there."

As soon as she stored her belongings, she glanced around, confused about where to go next. An older black lady with white hair gave her a toothy smile and pointed toward a metal door with a sign posted above that read "Visitors Holding Room."

Claire gave her a token nod of gratitude and followed a crowd of people moving in that direction. After passing through the metal detector, she was patted down by another female officer, who smelled of cigarettes and maple syrup. "Wait over there," the woman said, pointing to metal chairs lined up against a pea-green wall in bad need of paint.

She nodded and scanned for an empty chair, then sat to wait.

A man moved past, mopping the floor. His shoes made a slight squeaky sound every time he sludged forward, slowly pulling the dirty-looking mop across the speckled linoleum floor.

Claire looked away, focusing instead on a fake philodendron wedged in the corner, a few feet away from a drinking fountain hanging from the wall. Anything to quiet the voices in her head. Especially Jana Rae's.

"What are you? Ten shades of stupid?" her friend had asked over the phone.

"Look, this is something I need to do," Claire explained.

"Claire, listen to me. This crazy idea is going to put you square on the wrong end of an intervention. You know what I mean? Haven't you been through enough already?"

That was one thing Claire loved about Jana Rae. Few people could truly be counted on in life. Her crazy friend with blazing red hair and a mouth snappy as a bullwhip had always been in her corner of the arena. Even now.

Claire leaned her head back against the cold, hard wall of the holding room, keeping her eyes closed so she wouldn't have to see countless young girls waiting to see their baby daddies. The sight was far too depressing. But then, she wasn't so different. A female who had stood by her man and looked the other way, failing to see things as they really were.

Funny how she'd always known the grass was green—but never needed to know how or why.

She gnawed on her bottom lip, a habit she'd taken up as of late.

"Claire Massey?"

The booming voice caused her to startle. Claire glanced about the room as if there might be another woman with that name. "Me?" she asked.

The woman officer with the clipboard heaved a sigh laced with boredom. "Your name Massey?"

She nodded and stood. She followed the officer through the door and down a long hallway with windowless walls the color of the dried mud lining the pond out at Legacy Ranch, the one she'd gazed out at each morning while sitting in the breakfast nook.

The woman led her through a heavy metal door into a room less than half the size of her bathroom at home. Granted, the bathroom had been much larger than most, but this space felt cramped nonetheless.

A barrier cut the room in half, the upper portion made of glass grimy with handprints. The scene was straight out of a television episode of *CSI*.

Claire turned to thank the officer, but she was now alone. Nervous, she slid into the empty chair on her side of the barrier.

And waited.

Claire told herself to breathe. Her heart pounded wildly, and by the time the door on the other side of the barrier creaked open, every nerve fiber in her body was charged. It would take next to nothing to spark tears.

She trained her eyes on the doorway and vowed not to cry. Not here.

Then he entered, appearing older, more tired than the last time she'd seen him. Perhaps resigned to his circumstances. But he still looked at her with the same eyes—the ones she'd gazed into that night all those years ago at the Burger Hut. And so many times since.

Tuck quickly moved to the window and took his seat. With a guard standing nearby, he placed his shackled palm against the glass and mouthed, "I love you."

Claire blinked several times before picking up the telephone receiver and motioning for him to do the same.

He scrambled for the phone at his side, as though it were a line to the life he'd left behind . . . to her. He quickly nestled the black handset against his ear.

"Claire." He said her name with a kind of reverence, a tone you'd use with someone you cherished.

Claire swallowed against the dryness of her throat. She looked into her husband's eyes and steeled herself.

"I want a divorce."

BUY A WOMAN OF FORTUNE NOW!